THE PROMISES OF OPHELIA BENNETT

Books by Cecil Murphey Include...

- The Promises of Ophelia Bennett (fiction)
- Writer to Writer: Lessons from a Lifetime of Writing
- Unleash the Writer Within
- 90 Minutes in Heaven *(with Don Piper)*
- A Walk through the Dark: How My Husband's 90 Minutes in Heaven Deepened My Faith *(by Cecil Murphey and Gary Roe)*
- Gifted Hands: The Ben Carson Story *(with Dr. Ben Carson)*
- Not Quite Healed: 40 Truths for Male Survivors of Childhood Sexual Abuse *(by Cecil Murphey and Gary Roe)*
- Saying Goodbye: Facing the Death of a Loved One *(by Cecil Murphey and Gary Roe)*
- I Believe in Healing: Real Stories from the Bible, History and today *(by Cecil Murphey and Twila Belk)*
- I Believe in Heaven: Real Stories from the Bible, History and today *(by Cecil Murphey and Twila Belk)*
- Making Sense When Life Doesn't: The Secrets of Thriving in Tough Times
- Heavenly Company: Entertaining Angels Unaware *(by Cecil Murphey and Twila Belk)*
- Knowing God, Knowing Myself: An Invitation to Daily Discovery
- When a Man You Love Was Abused: A Woman's Guide to Helping Him Overcome Childhood Sexual Molestation
- When Someone You Love No Longer Remembers
- Because You Care: Spiritual Encouragement for Caregivers *(by Cecil Murphey and Twila Belk)*

THE PROMISES OF OPHELIA BENNETT

CECIL MURPHEY

The Promises of Ophelia Bennett

Published in the U.S. by:
OakTara Publishers
www.oaktara.com

Cover design by Yvonne Parks at www.pearcreative.ca
Cover image, antique books stacked on school desk © www.shutterstock.com: Holly Kuchera, 2007606.

Published in association with: Deidre Knight of The Knight Agency, Inc., 570 East Avenue, Madison, GA 30650; http://www.knightagency.net/.

ISBN-13: 978-1-60290-377-7
ISBN-10: 1-60290-377-8

Printed in the USA.

Prologue

Waukegan, Illinois, 1981

MICHAEL HEGE KNEW IT WASN'T TOO EARLY to go inside, but still he hesitated.

Twilight pressed its purple face against the windows of Rose Savantino's Ristorante. As its soft hues faded, darkness gently descended like a giant cape of weightless black silk.

The air had cooled and sent the smell of rain downward. He paused and studied the sky, assuring himself that he could meet the others.

For several seconds, Michael stared at the front door of the restaurant. The dimly lighted building gave the impression of smallness and intimacy, although they had several dining areas and a large reception room in the rear. He had been there twice before and remembered the fragrance of Mediterranean food that greeted his nostrils when he opened the door. Each table was covered with a light pink damask cloth and a slender vase held a single long-stemmed rose. This was the owner's trademark.

Tightness gripped his stomach and dampness spread under his armpits. This was the evening he had anticipated since Boy Masters had sent everyone the invitation two months earlier. This was also the evening he dreaded.

Michael pulled the folded invitation from his shirt pocket and stared at it, as if reading it for the first time. Not that he didn't know the time well enough, but he needed another reassuring glance at the printed words.

I wonder if she'll recognize me without the prominent freckles? It seemed strange to think of that, but at North Prairie School everyone had referred to him as the freckle-faced kid. He still carried the telltale marks, but his tanned skin and the first wrinkle lines made them less noticeable.

He closed his eyes, trying to visualize what Ophelia Bennett, his all-time favorite teacher, would look like today. His sandy hair now flecked with gray made him realize that she must have lost that titian color years ago. He hadn't seen Ophelia Bennett since she left North Prairie School. Although they had written regularly and she had phoned him many times, they had never met again in person.

"It's been my fault," he mumbled to himself. "For too long I was ashamed to see her."

Beyond the shame, he was also afraid. She would have seen the truth in his eyes—the way she always had. After he had straightened out his life, he told himself that he didn't know how to tell her. Yet, deep within himself, Michael was sure she knew—the way she seemed always to know how he felt or thought.

Several weeks after Mrs. Bennett left North Prairie, Michael's father had received a promotion contingent on relocation, so Michael and his family moved to Southern California. Even though he had been in Illinois a half-dozen times over the years, he had never gone to see his former teacher.

"I should have...," he said aloud.

Yes, you should have, his thoughts echoed.

I've known her for forty years. Forty years, and I can't remember a single day in my life that she hasn't been somewhere in my thoughts.

"You were always there—somewhere—calling out to me, praying for me, weren't you?" he whispered to the darkness.

How many times had he heard her voice when he faced a serious decision? when temptation knocked at the door? when confusion made him unable to make decisions? when self-pity or self-disgust paralyzed him? Those were the times he had heard her voice most clearly inside his head.

Despite that, Michael had pushed away her voice for several years, especially during the period he now referred to as the drunken years.

"You were always there."

Aware of the dampness on his cheeks, he brushed away the tears. He was sober, and he had been for the past twenty-three years. None of the others had known about that period. No one ever needed to know, not even Ophelia Bennett.

Michael straightened his tie, breathed deeply several times, and walked inside Rose Savantino's Ristorante. The lighting was warm. Recorded opera music played from carefully hidden speakers, loud enough to be heard but not intrusive. He smiled as he recognized Pavarotti's voice.

A couple brushed past him and approached the maître d'. After a few words and several obsequious smiles from the maître d', a waiter appeared and ushered them to a table close to where Michael stood. He turned his back on the maître d', not quite ready to go inside yet.

"...duck paté with cold Tay salmon and you finish your sumptuous meal with fresh strawberries coated in thick cream," the waiter said with such enthusiasm that Michael understood why people enjoyed Rose Savantino's.

Unable to delay his entrance any longer, Michael turned and walked forward.

The tuxedoed maître d' looked up and smiled. "Welcome to—"

"I'm here for a special party for—"

"The Ophelia Bennett party?"

"Yes, that's right. I'm a few minutes early." He chuckled self-consciously. "Are any others here yet?"

"Are there others here?" The maître d' nodded with a glint of humor in his eye. "But of course. They began to arrive by 6:30. One gentleman was standing at the door when we opened at 6:00."

"I suppose we're all a little anxious. This is—this is quite an important event to us."

Instead of calling a waiter, the maître d' gestured for Michael to follow him down a long hallway. After a couple of steps, he stopped and turned toward Michael. "Excuse me, sir. I have no right to ask this of you, but—"

"Sure, what is it?"

"This—this Ophelia Bennett. Is that a person or a corporation?" he asked with the faintest hint of an Italian accent. "Perhaps it is an institution. Never have I heard of it before."

"You might say it's an institution." Michael laughed. "No, actually, she is a teacher—my favorite teacher."

"Ahh, I see. For you to honor her this way, she must have for you taught many, many years."

"You could say it that way." Michael smiled to himself as he replayed the maître d's statement. "Yes, many years—and some of them were hard, almost impossible times. Yes, many, many years."

Instead of replying, the maître d' cocked his head, confusion written on his face.

"We never had another teacher like her. I'll tell you something else. She stayed in contact with us through the years. With every one of us—can you imagine that?"

"So many students? Frankly, sir, no, that I cannot—"

"You'd never understand, I suppose. Not unless you had been one of us. We've loved that woman—almost worshiped her—and we've continued to feel that way since the day I met her forty years ago." Michael chuckled to himself. "Well, I didn't feel that way in the beginning. Certainly not the first day—"

"Indeed, sir, she must be a most remarkable person," the uniformed man replied as they continued down the hallway.

"Remarkable," Michael repeated to himself. "That word seems hardly

adequate."

Ahead, Michael saw the large room. Even though the massive double oak doors were closed, happy voices carried into the hallway. He glanced at his watch: 7:24.

"Then I trust that this will be a most special time for all of you." He bowed his head and reached toward the door.

"That's fine. I, uh, I'll go in a second."

The man retreated down the hallway.

As Michael hesitated, he remembered the second promise that Mrs. Bennett had made to them. That was the primary reason he had come tonight. The fulfillment of that promise had changed the course of his life.

1

Northern Illinois, 1940

OPHELIA BENNETT PULLED HER 1937 FORD to the side of the road and shut off the engine. She stared at her shaking hands, willing them to relax. "I can't go through this. Not again. Oh, God, please, please not again."

The first leaves of fall swirled lazily from the red maples and massive oaks. On another day, she would have gazed in awe at the patina of color falling on the hood of her black car. A threshing machine chugged monotonously in the distance and made its presence known by the faint aroma of wheat straw that filled the air.

It was the day after Labor Day. As it had every year, school would start this morning. Ophelia peered at the road as if she could see the two more miles ahead, a wide turn, and the long, brick building enclosed by a large metal fence.

"Is there no other way for me? Is this—is this what I must do for you?" As she spoke the words, Ophelia Bennett knew the answer. "Start the engine and go on," she commanded herself.

"Not yet; oh, I cannot. God, give me the strength. Without that, I cannot go through this." She leaned her head back against the seat, and for a long time her eyes saw nothing and her lips moved in silent prayer.

No matter how she tried to divert her thoughts, Mr. Pettygill's words stole control. Only five days earlier she had sat in the county superintendent's office. The Lake County school district had been her last chance for a position to teach. Every other school district had filled their quota before June.

Sylvester Pettygill had several positions available and she had hoped for one in Zion or Waukegan. He had offered her nothing that suited her education and background. She had not taught for the past three years, and he labored to make her aware of her need to be grateful.

For the first twenty minutes of the interview, even when his voice grew forceful, Mr. Pettygill's face never changed expression. "I generously offer you this position," he said, winding down, "for one major reason. It is because I am fully confident that you can handle North Prairie School. Your exemplary record makes that obvious." He paused and leaned forward. "I have assigned you as principal and teacher of grades one through four at North Prairie School."

"North Prairie. Surely not—"

"Yes, it is a demanding position—very demanding. However, I assume you will readily agree and allow this to be a stepping stone to a more, uh, rewarding position."

"You mean, then, that I have no choice."

"Of course, you have a choice," he said. "You do not have to return to teaching."

"I—we—have—I need to work. My husband—"

"Yes, yes, yes, I know, and I wish to help you, which is precisely the reason I am willing to offer you a position one week before the school year begins." For the first time, his face made an unsuccessful attempt to smile. "I trust you will defer to my judgment and accept this as a challenge to your vast and well-proven techniques. You have rare talents and the ability to—"

Ophelia Bennett's blue eyes remained fixed on his gaunt face and the words went past her without registering. She had heard his lavish flattery too often the past few days for it to have any effect.

He stopped talking and studied his finely manicured nails for an interminable time before he cleared his throat. "The truth is, we need someone of your caliber there." He softened his voice, another technique she had previously witnessed. "This temporary assignment requires the best teacher I have available. *I need you*, Mrs. Bennett, but more important, North Prairie needs you."

"I am not certain if I can." As she spoke those words, Ophelia dropped her head. A startling premonition streaked through her mind. She did not doubt that invasive understanding—it had come to her too often in the past.

"Of course you can do it. You need not be modest. I know better and I know of your excellent record in Lake County before your marriage. Yes, my dear Mrs. Bennett, with your background and your uncanny grasp of—" His words continued flowing but Ophelia had stopped listening again.

She knew about the students at North Prairie, or at least she had heard about them. So had every teacher in the county system. Even though it was a two-room, two-teacher school, its reputation had spread everywhere. Her hesitancy had nothing to do with her ability to get them under control or to teach them. "I had hoped not to be in such a place again—"

"Yes, yes, yes, I do understand; however, under more normal circumstances, you would be one of the few teachers I would never dare to ask," he said. "The fact is, I have no one else available. With budgets the way they are, we cannot possibly hire more teachers. I did not have to hire you. As a matter of fact, in issuing you a contract—" He held up the two pages so she could see that he had not yet signed. "In fact, uh, as you may be aware, you are the last teacher hired under our current budget—"

"So you have said several times."

"I have taken up your cause, as you know. I am solidly behind you. Do not forget that I have taken up your cause."

"Then, out of gratefulness, I should acquiesce."

Not catching the caustic note in her voice, he wrote his name on the contract. "Yes, that is what I consider the proper response." He signed a second copy and handed it to her. "You do understand that I made this decision not without opposition. One, uh, influential person reminded me of the, uh, problems in Bentonville. You received this position only because I intervened for you."

"Out of kindness?" she asked, knowing he would miss the irony of the question.

"Most assuredly. Of course, it was also because of your exemplary record."

"I do not wish to teach at North Prairie. Please, is there not some other place?"

"North Prairie is where I need you." Their eyes locked and he said, "All right, I shall be brutally frank with you. Either you teach or we simply have to close North Prairie. We cannot do that to the children, can we? As I said, the children need you."

The children. Yes, she thought and inwardly shuddered. Having gone through this kind of situation before, she remembered only too well how such undisciplined children drained her stamina. *Oh, dear Lord,* she prayed silently, *why do I have to do this again?* Yet even as she asked, Ophelia knew she had no choice. She could accomplish what other teachers could not.

Even more important, she would love those needy children, and they would respond to that love. That was part of her gift to them. She also remembered the jealous reactions of other teachers. Worse, of course, would be the reaction of the community.

That she could change conditions in the school, she had no doubt. She had done that before. *It is so difficult,* she said to herself, *with so many misunderstandings and jealousies. Oh, must I do this yet again?*

Ophelia had heard from others that at least two other teachers had refused. "I would resign from the profession before I would go there," one woman had said.

"They are terrible, stupid, stupid children," another said, "and it is a thankless environment. No one stays long. Most of them stick it out until the end of the first year and then move on."

Yes, she knew about North Prairie.

As Mr. Pettygill prattled on about her talents and the need, he carefully avoided the one argument that would force her to take the position. She had taught for nine years before she married, and in those days, when a woman married, she was forced to leave the system. He knew about Richard and their financial circumstances, and why she had chosen to return to the field. If she did well at North Prairie, he could open doors for her to continue teaching in better-paying positions. And he would follow through. That much she knew about him. But if she refused, he would see that she would not teach again in Illinois.

"Give me two days to ponder this. I want to be certain that it is the best place for me." She did not know why she stalled unless it was so that Mr. Pettygill could not experience a total victory.

"I had expected an immediate response." His eyes bored into hers.

Ophelia Bennett said nothing more. *I refuse to be intimidated by silence or that demanding gaze. You have won, but I will not make it easy for you.*

"Very well. This is Tuesday. I'll be in my office at 8:00 on Thursday; I shall expect your acceptance call by 8:45."

"*If* I accept," she said. "Is that not the purpose of my having time to reflect on this?"

"Uh, yes, of course, of course." He cleared his throat again. "I know you well enough to be fully persuaded that you will make the correct decision."

*

Two days later, Ophelia Bennett called Mr. Pettygill's office. "I have decided to accept the position at North Prairie."

"Very wise, and very, very compassionate of you," he said. "Oh, and yes, uh, something else, unfortunately, that I must tell you. Miss Perkins, the other teacher, is ill. Quarantined with mumps yesterday. That means, of course, I will expect you to handle all the children."

"All of them? What about a substitute? You are asking an enormous amount—"

"For any other teacher, I would search high and low for a substitute. However, aside from budget limitations, I am fully confident that you can handle all thirty-three of them easily enough. After all, it is only for two weeks, or, uh, perhaps three." As Sylvester Pettygill spoke, Ophelia could not mistake his gloating tone. "I know you can handle all of them—both classes. My dear Mrs. Bennett, you are that kind of exemplary teacher. You can do it."

"If she is ill, I do not have a choice," she said more to herself.

"Quite right. Thank you." Mr. Pettygill hung up.

*

"This is unfair," she now said to the silence of the car. "Unfair." She had expected to teach the younger children, which was demanding and draining enough, but not to teach every child at North Prairie from first through eighth grade. Of course, she had done that during her early years of teaching.

Tears trickled down her face, but Ophelia hardly noticed. "I have signed the contract, and I am obligated to do it. Oh, God, I need wisdom—and strength—a lot of strength." She rested her head on the steering wheel.

"Need some help?"

Ophelia jerked her head up and saw the young man who stood next to her car, one foot on the running board. "No, uh, no, I—I only pulled over for a minute."

"I saw your car and you leaning over the wheel. I thought maybe you were sick or something. I'll be glad to help if—"

"Thank you," she said, her voice now under control. "I shall be fine."

"Are you sure? I mean, I could follow—"

"Really, no. It was thoughtful of you to stop, but I am quite all right." She smiled, suddenly conscious of her tear-streaked cheeks.

The young man shrugged and returned to his new Packard. As he got inside, he waved at her. She waved back and waited. He didn't start his car.

She sighed. "I assume he will stay here as long as I do." Pushing her foot on the starter until the engine turned over and caught, she then let out the clutch, shifted, and pulled back onto the road. She waved her thanks again. Only then did he start his car, follow behind her for a short distance, and after half a mile, race ahead. As soon as his Packard had vanished around a curve, Ophelia stopped the car again. She took out her handkerchief and carefully wiped her cheeks. She checked her face in the mirror and straightened her bobbed red hair.

"I am ready now—as ready as I can be. God, you must help me." She started the engine once again, pressed on the clutch and shifted into first gear. Leaving the state highway, she turned right on North Prairie Road.

2

EVERY CHILD TURNED TO WATCH THE 1937 FORD coming down the dirt road, still a long way off. Not many cars traveled the paved roads in that part of Lake County, Illinois, in 1940—fewer still on the dirt roads. They watched the late-summer dust fly in billowing clouds as the car sped toward its destination. No one shouted and no one whispered. Silently, every child stood with face pressed against the fence, waiting for the first glimpse of the new teacher. They knew that Miss Perkins was coming back, and they didn't understand why, because they had made her miserable the previous year. The eighth graders insisted she was coming back only because she couldn't get a teaching job anywhere else.

The black Ford pulled slowly into the school driveway before it stopped at the left side of the building. Seconds later, even though it seemed much longer, a tall, slim woman got out.

Ophelia Bennett was forty-six years old, but because of her poised gait and her inner confidence, most people assumed she was older. She wore a white blouse with a princess collar, a straight, black skirt, and dark silk stockings. The first strands of silver glinted from her titian hair. She carried a large black purse in her left hand.

"Bet she's taller'n my dad." A third-grade boy nudged a companion. "'Bout the tallest teacher I ever seen."

"Bet she's not as tall as my dad," his friend chimed defensively.

"Lookit that red hair!" gasped an eighth-grade girl as the thin figure walked from the car to the school door.

Mrs. Bennett climbed the four steps, paused at the door, and then—as if she previously had been unaware of their presence—turned toward thirty-two pairs of gawking eyes. "Good morning," she said.

The voice sounded neither harsh nor kind. She didn't smile; she didn't frown either. By now the students, especially those in fourth grade and above, had learned to size up new teachers. If she smiled (like "toothy Miss Green with the long nose"), it signaled she wanted to be friendly. Her opening statement would begin with something silly such as, "Boys and girls, we want to be one happy family here at North Prairie."

If she frowned, the children knew it meant she would be a stern disciplinarian, who tolerated no nonsense. She would make them sit stiffly at their desks and allow no slumping over, moving around, or talking. That kind didn't seem to care if they learned anything, just so they sat quietly. That was the kind who found the air let out of her tires, the toilet paper stolen from the girl's lavatory, and ink mysteriously blotting out her assignment book when she arrived at school.

The type of teacher didn't matter to the pupils at North Prairie School. Strict or friendly, they provided easy targets for the children to defeat. This redheaded beanpole would be no exception. Their silent faces, nudging gestures, and occasional whisper affirmed agreement as their gaze followed Mrs. Bennett into the school.

Ten minutes after arriving, the new teacher rang the school bell and the children filed in. Some smiled, others scowled, all scrutinized the new teacher to decide which tactics to use.

"Please find seats—everyone—in this classroom. Miss Perkins is ill today," the redheaded teacher said. "I'll be teaching all eight grades."

They stared, still sizing her up, and waited. Despite her order to take any seat, they knew that couldn't be correct.

"Sit down."

They raced for seats, filling the back row first. The younger children ended up closest to her.

"Because Miss Perkins is ill, everyone will remain in this classroom until she returns."

"What's wrong with her?" Michael Hege, a freckle-faced first grader, raised his hand at the same time he asked. "She didn't decide to die or something, did she?"

"She has mumps."

"Mumps?"

The word reverberated throughout the room. Children puffed out their cheeks and gawked at each other. Snickers continued a long time after the room had begun to settle down again.

Mrs. Bennett sat quietly and waited for silence. Then she spoke in a voice so soft that every child had to lean slightly forward to hear what she said. "I have heard you are the stupidest and most ill-behaved children in the whole of Lake County. Do you like being branded *stupid?*"

"Well, ah is very stupid," Marvin Bagnull said, crossing his eyes as he spread his mouth open at the corners with each hand and wiggled his ears.

"No, young man, only rude," snapped the teacher as she lurched from her desk, grabbed Marvin by the scuff of his neck, and yanked him out of his seat.

"We shall have sufficient time for playing games. This is not one of those times." She dropped him back into his seat.

Ophelia Bennett walked around the room and stared at each child as if evaluating him or her. She had not raised her voice when she grabbed Marvin, and the softness of her words made them even more forceful. The children watched quietly, aware only of the tapping of her Cuban-heeled shoes as she moved across the hardwood floor.

She continued staring.

Nickolas Harrison, already six feet tall, grew impatient with the inspection and marked on his desktop with a pencil. As though she had been awaiting the signal, Ophelia Bennett darted to the boy's desk and snatched the pencil from his hand. "And what, young man, are you doing?"

The coldness of her voice made a freckle-faced first-grader sob.

No one paid any attention to him. All eyes stared at Nickolas Harrison, who had once knocked down a teacher. No one could remember that teacher's name—she had lasted only four days.

"I repeat, what are you doing?" The now stern voice permeated the room.

No one moved, mesmerized by the tall figure that faced Nickolas squarely and refused to glance away. Even the freckle-faced boy stopped sobbing and watched.

"Aw, just markin' on my desk, I guess."

"Either you know or you do not know what you were doing. We shall have no guesswork here. Now, again, what were you doing?" The blue eyes had become two tiny rays of piercing light directed at the muscular boy.

"Markin' on my desk," he replied coldly, trying to turn his face away, yet seemingly unable to do so.

The children noticed his fists doubling up. Besides being the largest and strongest boy in the class, Nickolas Harrison also became angry the fastest. His temper scared the younger children.

"Marking. Please say it again with the 'g' at the end of the word."

"Marking! Marking! Marking!"

Most of the children gasped.

"Correct. Apparently you enjoy destroying property. However, you are destroying property that is not yours. That desk belongs to the school and to the community. We shall have no more of this. After school, you will wash down *every* desk with soap and water before you return to your home." Her eyes, oblivious to the clenched fists, continued boring into Nickolas's eyes.

"Every desk?" he shrieked in unbelief.

"Your hearing is normal," replied the cold voice that originated below the piercing eyes. "I assume your intelligence at least matches. But you do not need to worry about the task you have been assigned. I shall remain here to instruct you on how to wash a desk properly."

"But—but it'll take all night!" protested the thirteen-year-old boy.

"Possibly, but I intend to remain until you finish. Yes, it will inconvenience me, but I have sufficient work to do."

Nickolas slumped in his desk.

In that fraction of a second, all of them knew their hero had been beaten. Nickolas knew it too and seemed dazed by it all.

Karen Whiting, also an eighth grader, glared at Ophelia Bennett. The teacher had berated Nickolas, whom she worshiped. Certain she could not be seen, Karen stuck out her tongue at Mrs. Bennett.

Catherine Murphy giggled, then ducked her head, afraid Mrs. Bennett would pounce on her.

The teacher continued to pace as she talked. "As I said earlier, you children have given this school a terrible reputation. You do not know how difficult—no, impossible—it is to get someone to teach at this school. Most teachers know how badly you have behaved here. But I think we can change that. Yes, I think we can change that," she said, almost as though talking to herself.

She stopped abruptly and moved her eyes up and down the rows. "Yes, I have made a decision. I have decided to give you children a choice. If you truly wish to maintain your reputation as perfectly horrible, disrespectful students, I can teach you to be absolutely perfect fiends. But only if you wish."

"What's a *fiend?*" the freckle-faced boy asked.

"A *fiend,*" the teacher said benevolently as she draped an arm around the boy, "is a term I use for the most mean, ill-tempered, naughty child. If that is all you wish to learn at school, we can decide that now and I shall teach you some terrible tricks—worse than any you have ever played before—and I can assure you that everyone will hate you."

She surveyed the room again. "Or," the low voice continued, "I can make you into the smartest and best-behaved children in the entire county."

"Ugh!" came a sound from the rear of the room.

"Yes, I cannot blame you for saying that. However, you did not allow me to finish my last statement. I can also assure you that you will have more fun than you have ever had. You will actually look forward to coming to school each day." She held up her hand before anyone could interrupt her. "If you choose this second option, and if we do not have a good time together, I promise that you may vote again and revert to your outlandish behavior."

"What's 'vert' mean?" the perpetual questioner asked.

The question went unanswered this time. Ophelia Bennett stopped in front of the room, directly alongside her desk. She shifted only her gaze, allowing it to bounce from head to head while the children stared back in complete silence.

"This ain't the way teachers are supposed to act," Larry Leech mumbled to no one in particular.

"You would not know about how teachers are supposed to behave, because you have never allowed them to teach or so I understand. I have also decided to do this fairly. For the next two weeks we shall work hard—at games and at having a good time. We want school to be fun, but it must be the right kind of fun. Now, I have only two conditions—"

She walked over to the freckle-faced boy who was getting ready to speak. "If you'll wait until later, I promise to make certain you understand. Now, sit quietly."

His eyes widened and he gulped, but he clamped his mouth shut. A few snickers circled the back of the room because it was common knowledge that the freckle-faced boy, at six years of age, had the undisputed reputation of being the most obnoxious child in the community. Mothers had often shaken their heads. "Whatever will he do when he gets to school?"

"As I said," Ophelia continued in her low, soft voice, "I have only two conditions. First, this is our classroom and we do not tell anyone outside the school building what we are doing—at least not during our two-week trial period. Is that clear?"

"You mean, like a secret?" Ginger Garrett blurted out.

"No, I do not mean *like* a secret; I mean a secret. This will be an agreement between you and me for two weeks—or until Miss Perkins returns. After all, two weeks is not long, and after that period of time you may vote to change everything back to your wild, unruly ways. Does everyone agree to that first condition?"

Heads nodded, a few voices mumbled yes with some uncertainty.

"Excellent. Now here is the second condition. During this two-week period we shall have no mean or practical jokes. No releasing air from my tires, no pouring motor oil into paint jars, no climbing in through the ceiling of the building and splashing my papers with ink."

From the corners of their eyes, children stole glances at one another. The quizzical expression went from pupil to pupil.

"How does she know?" Karen silently formed the words as she looked across the row at Nickolas.

Nickolas shrugged as if he were saying he was in no mood for conversation or lip reading.

"Of course, I have to promise you something, too, would you not agree? My promise is to make learning fun. We shall allow normal amounts of noise and you may move around. I shall also allow you to spend extra time on the projects you enjoy doing. That is, if you agree to my two conditions."

She stared silently around the room, waiting for a response from each child. None of them knew how to respond.

"Since no one has disagreed, I assume everyone will abide by this decision."

She walked over to Nickolas's desk and peered into the sulking brown eyes. "Young man, I would like you to do me a favor. Please."

He looked up in disbelief.

"You appear strong and probably quite intelligent. You also look like a leader. I have the trunk and back seat of my vehicle filled with materials for use this morning. Will you select three boys to help you bring them in? I assume that I can depend on you to see that nothing gets broken."

Nickolas flashed Ophelia Bennett a grin. "Sure, sure." He hopped from his seat, called three names, and said in a commanding tone, "All right, let's bring everything in carefully."

Karen smiled at Mrs. Bennett now and showed her even teeth. Nickolas caught her smile as he headed out the door.

While the boys carried in the six boxes and four packages, Ophelia Bennett moved her own desk into a corner, away from the row of windows. "All right, you may sit at any desk you please for the time being *and* you may move your desk to any spot in the room. We will not worry about rows."

Children scuffled and moved desks around, changing two or three times. They began to whisper and then talk in quiet tones. At the same time they watched the teacher closely, their attention diverted by the boys carrying the boxes into the room. Only Max Waxman and Masters remained in their seats. Neither showed any inclination to move or acted as though he had heard.

When everything had been carried in and piled in front of the classroom next to her desk, Ophelia stood. "Thank you very much. You have done an excellent job," she said to Nickolas. "And you did it quite rapidly too. Thank you. I know we shall have an excellent time together."

Nickolas blushed, bowed his head slightly, and walked back to his desk. He caught Karen's adoring smile as he passed her desk.

"I want this seat by the window," the freckle-faced boy screamed at an older girl. "I like this seat and you can't have it!"

"I sat here first while you tried out a seat on the other side of the room," the girl yelled back.

"Did not!"

"You did so, you baby!"

Michael screamed. He doubled his fists and pounded on the desk.

Ophelia Bennett grabbed the boy's shoulders and glared into his face. "Your screaming will get you nowhere in my classroom. She is quite right—you first chose the other side of the room. Now sit there!"

"Won't!"

"Do as I say."

"Can't make me. I'll tell my mother!"

Ophelia Bennett swatted the boy on the buttocks and he moved quickly across the room.

"I hate you," he mumbled under his breath.

"And now," her voice even once again, "we are ready to start. Before coming here, I read the achievement scores of all of you who have been here previously. Frankly, as you well know, they are terrible. They indicate that only one of you, including the eighth graders, can read on a level beyond the second grade. We shall change that immediately."

She walked over to the pile of materials, picked up a long narrow box, and laid it on her desk. "We shall start with a game. It is one I invented and I have used it before, quite successfully. This morning everyone in the class—all eight grades—will start to read at the same place...right at the beginning. After our first lesson, I shall assign you to teams—not by your age or regular grade but by the way you catch on to the game."

None of the students looked at each other, although frowns and question marks appeared on most faces. As she opened the box, she said, "This first game I call my Monkey Ladder. It is because you will all sound a little like monkeys as you learn to pronounce the short vowels." She wrote the vowels on the blackboard. "It will take me about four minutes to explain, and after that we'll play. It goes like this..."

3

"I HAVE REFLECTED ON YESTERDAY'S PROGRESS. It is quite fortunate for me that there are no stupid children in this classroom." Ophelia Bennett sighed as she made her first statement the second morning of school. "I am immensely relieved, because you will make my task much easier. However, I have spotted a few lazy, misdirected, and undisciplined children."

The children stared at her as she stepped from behind her worn mahogany desk.

"Yes, this school will be easier to work with than I had originally thought. You see, I expected several stupid children, but you have surpassed my expectations. For one thing, every one of you is above average in intelligence."

Mrs. Bennett circled the room and called several students by name to commend them on their excellent work the day before. "Yes, it is most gratifying to realize that you are quite intelligent." She paused at the desk of a constantly squinting Max, a tall, thin boy with light-brown hair combed straight forward except for the cowlick that resembled a small feather. He dropped his head. "That includes you, Max."

His head shot up and his cold glare called her a liar.

"Yes, Max, even you."

Students stared quizzically at one another. Didn't Mrs. Bennett know who he was? Max Waxman. "Waxie Maxie has wax in his ears!" the children taunted when they chased him on the playground.

"Dumb Max has lots of wax!" was the first line of a favorite sing-songy tune they had made up.

The boy had learned to ignore their words and taunts. The more they teased, the more silent he became in their presence.

Across from Max sat his only friend, Masters, who glowered at the teacher. "Your dumb tricks won't work with us," he said. "I'm ugly and Max is dumb."

The children had songs about Masters, too.

"You will prove to yourselves that I have spoken truthfully." Mrs. Bennett smiled at Max and Masters and resumed moving around the classroom.

The freckle-faced boy snickered.

"When I consider the progress you students made yesterday, I know I can give you the annual achievement tests before Christmas—" She halted long enough to smile down at the freckle-faced boy and said, almost as an aside, "Annual means something done each year."

He nodded.

She turned back to the class and added, "You do not believe me now, but you will. You will easily outscore the city children in Lake County. I have faith in you. Usually, we wait until late spring to give this test, but you will be ready—*every one of you.*"

"Did we do well yesterday?" Marvin asked. "Honest to truth, did we?"

"All of you did so well yesterday—even the first graders—that you have already completed the work I had prepared for three days."

The students looked even more perplexed. No teacher had ever talked that way before. What did they do next? Several sneaked glances at Nickolas. The second day at school traditionally meant the beginning of organized rebellion. Nickolas ignored them.

Karen, who sat beside him, poked his arm and raised an eyebrow. Her lips formed the question, "What's wrong?"

Nickolas turned away and smiled at Mrs. Bennett.

"You force me to work diligently—quite diligently—to stay ahead of you," the teacher said. "Yesterday I taught you the Monkey Ladder. You learned to sound out many words. You did extremely well, especially because many of the words you have not had in your reading books before. Even more impressive, you can now read most of the required words for your grade levels. Yes, I am impressed with your learning pace."

Quizzical gestures morphed to smiles. Max and Masters exchanged grins. Marvin beamed.

"You may review the spelling words now, using the blackboards, and Marvin will read the words." The boards covered two full walls of the building. "There is enough space and chalk for everyone to work." She nodded at the class and walked to the back of the room.

The children stared at one another for a moment, but none moved.

Are we free to go to the blackboard? their silent faces asked.

"We never went to the board before," Marvin said. "I mean, not all of us at once. Miss Perkins says it's too messy and Miss Kapoozie said..."

"I am Mrs. Bennett. All of you may go to the board. Now."

An immediate scuffling and pushing preceded a shoving for places, erasers, and chalk. By understanding the sound of short vowels the previous day, every child had learned to spell between five and fifteen words. Marvin pronounced the first one, "Bat."

Chalk scratched the word on the board and the children waited.

"Apple," he said.

Ophelia Bennett seemed not to notice them, because she focused her attention on Max, who had not moved from his seat.

"You think you are stupid. Is it true that you think so, Max?"

He shook his head affirmatively.

"Do you like being labeled *stupid?"*

"No, 'course not," he whispered. "The others laugh at me, but I can't help it. I do the best I can." Tears sprang to his eyes, and he turned his head away from her.

"I am so pleased to hear your answer. It should be no trouble working with you. Some people enjoy being stupid. But you do not. Yes, I like that. You are quite sensitive; you feel things easily. You will be remarkably easy to teach."

The hardened expression returned to the boy's thin face.

Ophelia laid her hand lightly on his shoulder. She smiled at him and said nothing until the hardness slowly melted.

"But I—" he began as his voice broke.

"You want to tell me I am mistaken. You may give me a variety of excuses for being stupid. They are, however, only excuses. You see, I already know you are not mentally deficient in any way. You are, as a matter of fact, quite bright—"

"Am not—"

As if he hadn't spoken, she said, "Therefore, from now on, I will not allow such thinking. An intelligent boy like you can be so easily lost to the world because you have been misdirected. You *are* intelligent."

He shook his head. "Not me," he mumbled.

"I watched how quickly you caught on yesterday. Had you been stupid, you would not have mastered those diphthongs. In fact, you were the first to learn them. Were you aware of that?"

He shook his head.

"The first one, Max."

"I don't want to be stupid, Mrs. Bennett, but I can't help it!" the boy said with desperation.

"That is the tone I wish to hear. Yes, Max, that is what I wish to hear. Now I am convinced I shall be able to help you." She smiled as if he had given her a pleasurable, unexpected response. "You are now ready to exercise your

God-endowed intelligence. This afternoon I shall write a note to your mother and father and insist they take you for an eye examination. Are you aware of your constant squinting?"

"Yes'm, 'cause I can't see well." For the first time, his eyes met hers. "But I'm taller than most of the others in the room, and the teachers always make me sit in back so the short ones can see everything. I can't see much and the teachers yell at me 'cause I don't know what's going on."

"You will not be embarrassed again."

Max looked down and played nervously with his fingers.

Larry, who had been listening carefully from the blackboard at the left side of the room, peeked around. Mrs. Bennett's gaze met his as she wiped tears from her eyes and turned quickly so no one else would see.

Masters had also stayed at his desk and kept his eyes diverted by staring at his English book.

"If I had magic powers to make you feel intelligent, Max, would you like that?"

He nodded cautiously.

"Excellent. I have three rules to make you the most brilliant boy in this school. First, it demands determination. Second, you must learn concentration, and third, it requires repetition. I shall enable you to develop all three."

"I don't know—"

She held up her hand. "It will not be as difficult as you fear. You supply the determination. I shall teach you to concentrate, and I promise you that you will catch on to the repetition and enjoy it."

The boy looked dubiously at his teacher, but he quietly said, "Thank you."

"You are very thin, Max, and I presume you do not eat much at meal times. Is that correct?"

"Yes—"

"Perhaps that is the way to approach your brilliant growth—and it will be brilliant. Yes, I think so. The way to do your schoolwork is to take on a little at a time. Instead of learning twenty spelling words, you may try eight. I'll teach you a few word games and simple tricks to help you learn how to cement those into your brain. Eight is all that I'll require of you until you have fully absorbed them. My assumption is that within two weeks, you will be eager to add more words."

"Will it work?" he asked.

"Of course! This will succeed because you and I shall focus on this together. Most importantly, when you cannot understand a problem or an assignment, you must come to me immediately. Do not hesitate to ask. You shall learn!"

Ophelia Bennett lightly squeezed Max's shoulder and then went back to the front of the classroom. She surveyed the board, and before anyone realized what had happened, she grabbed the freckle-faced boy by the scruff of the neck. "You were playing at this board—but you were not practicing your spelling words that Marvin pronounced!"

"I—I couldn't find an eraser. Ginger wouldn't give me an eraser—"

Ophelia Bennett shook the boy sharply several times. "Listen carefully, Michael, and do not talk back to me. You are selfish and spoiled and you have gotten your way at home and with everyone else. You will not be pampered in this classroom. Is that clear?"

Although she had jerked the boy around to face her, she held firmly to the scruff of his neck.

"You're hurting my neck!" he squealed.

"That is not likely. However, you are avoiding my question. Do you understand me?"

"It hurts. I'll tell my daddy! He's on the school board and—"

With her left hand she reached out and swatted the freckle-faced boy on the seat of his pants. "I will have none of that. You cannot frighten me. I made it clear to Mr. Pettygill when I accepted this job that I would spank if and when necessary. And, young man, I shall not release you until we have an understanding. *Now answer me.*"

Even though fear etched the boy's face, he stared defiantly at Ophelia Bennett. Every child stopped, caught up in the tension between the nearly six-foot-tall redheaded teacher and Michael. She waited silently, not releasing her grasp on the boy's collar.

Karen suppressed a giggle, Ginger gasped, and Nickolas smiled. The others either stared or furtively punched each other.

The large clock in the back of the room ticked as it moved to the next minute. A second minute passed before Ophelia Bennett saw the boy's answer. A trickle of urine wove its way slowly across the hardwood floor.

"He wet himself!" Karen squealed. "How stinky!" she said and covered her nose, even though she could not possibly have smelled it.

"You made me do it!" the boy shouted. "It's your fault. And I'm going to tell on you."

Mrs. Bennett stared at the boy but said nothing.

Quickly changing tactics, Michael began to sob.

The teacher didn't release him. "Which method works better for you at home? Yelling? Crying? Wetting yourself? I assume you have perfected such methods." She held him tightly and watched the trickle continue across the floor. The front of his overalls was soaked.

"Let me go!" His gaze shifted from his pants to the teacher's face to the small rivulet of urine. He started to scream, but she did not release him, so he increased the volume of his sobs.

"When you have finished your tantrum, I am certain we shall find other clothes for you to change into," she said.

His crying stopped immediately and he stared at her in disbelief. "I hate you and I want out of here—and—and—I have—I have to go home and change my pants."

"Oh, no, not in my school! I am certain we can find something else for you to put on." She pulled him to her supply closet and pointed. "Pick up the pasteboard box."

He hesitated and she tightened her grip. He picked up the box.

"You will find whatever you need in there—discarded clothing left here at North Prairie."

Dragging him behind her, she swooped past her desk and headed for the boys' lavatory.

*

From inside the classroom the others heard only noises and muffled sounds. The freckle-faced boy started crying again. "You can't make me do that! I won't!"

They also heard the distinctive sound of a hand swatting bare flesh.

The crying stopped.

*

Mrs. Bennett pulled out the box Michael held. "These are discarded articles of clothing from previous students." She held up a pair of bib overalls.

"Too big. 'Sides, they belonged to David Rosenberry. He lived next door to me, and nobody liked him and he moved away."

"Oh, I see." She had started to sort through the pasteboard box and stopped. "You may go through the contents. Put on whatever you feel is appropriate."

"What's approp—"

"Put on whatever you like and return to the classroom."

He stared into her eyes. "I hate you more than anyone else in the whole world."

"Thank you," she said. "Even though you are rude, I do not dislike you." She nudged the box toward him.

*

A few minutes later the first grader walked slowly into the classroom. He glowered at the teacher, but she made no response. He dropped his head, hesitating as if he wanted to return to the boys' lavatory before he stepped forward again. He stared straight in front of him as he headed toward his desk. Giggles filled the classroom.

"Lookit the baby!" Nickolas shouted in his soon-to-become-bass voice.

"Want to sit on my lap, baby?" Marvin called out. "But then, you might wet yourself again and I'd get all soaked!"

Michael wore a large diaper, secured to his shirt by two large safety pins. He sat at his desk and slumped forward.

"Enough! He chose to wear the diaper. He has embarrassed himself and we will not add to his humiliation." Her gaze moved from face to face to make certain everyone understood. "We shall have no more laughing at him. I believe he has learned a valuable lesson. Now we are ready to play a new game."

"Max. Masters. Michael. Go to the board."

The diapered boy shook his head.

"You have had a difficult moment, but it is not anything you will need to repeat. You may put this behind you and you will enjoy learning."

The teacher waited. Max and Masters went to the board.

"I like you very much, Michael. In fact, I like you so much that I will *not* allow you to continue in your childish ways. *Go to the board."*

Michael took his place next to Max.

"Today, you will discover how easily you can learn your multiplication tables," she said in her calm voice. "You will learn without groaning over having to memorize them."

4

AT 10:49, THE SCHOOL DOOR OPENED A FEW INCHES. At first Ophelia assumed the brisk wind had forced open the heavy oak door. Another inch filled the room with a creaking sound. *Too regular to be the wind,* Ophelia thought and fixed her gaze on the door. So did thirty-two pairs of eyes.

A Mexican girl, about ten years of age, stepped slowly forward. Silently, the elfin figure took two more steps. Her coal-black hair, neatly parted in the middle and tightly braided in pigtails, complemented her dark complexion. Her loose-fitting dress, now faded beyond recognizable color, had once been either blue or green. A dark-green patch was neatly sewed across the waist. Socks hung loosely across the top of her obviously too-large shoes. Enormous black eyes stared from the tiny boned girl as she eased herself toward the corner of the room.

"Yes? Come in, please," Mrs. Bennett said warmly. "May I help you?"

"That's just Yvonne Ortega!" Marvin snickered. "She moved away, and we didn't think she'd move back here. Anyway, she only comes to school half the time."

"She lives in a shack behind our house," Karen said. "Her father works for us, so we let them live there."

Someone else snickered too.

"And she's dumb! Real dumb!" called out second-grader James, who had pulled out his first tooth that morning and resulted in his having a slight lisp. "She gets her sums wrong every time!"

"Come in, my dear," Ophelia Bennett said, still seated at her desk.

The small figure moved slightly forward, stopped, turned around, and shut the door. She took several steps into the room and gasped. A bewildered look covered her face. Four students sat in one corner doing art projects. Another group, huddled in the north section of the room, studied butterflies with a magnifying glass.

"I—I don't know to sit where...," mumbled Yvonne with a thick accent.

"Buenos dias, Yvonne. *Como esta usted?"*

"Muy bien, gracias," the wide-eyed girl replied.

Ophelia Bennett held out her arm, beckoning Yvonne to the only empty desk. The girl smiled and showed even white teeth. She threw her head back and walked to the empty desk. Mrs. Bennett took Yvonne's right hand and shook it. *"Permita usted que me presente, Senora Bennett."*

"Mucho gusto en conocerla," the girl said brightly. (I'm glad to know you).

"Habla usted Englis?" the teacher asked. (Do you speak English?)

"Un poco," mumbled the girl. (A little.)

"Hey, Mrs. Bennett, how do you know Spanish?" James asked.

"Love speaks many languages," Mrs. Bennett said to the students, "and there are no barriers to communication with love." She turned to the freckle-faced boy and said, "Communication means conversation or talking between people."

"Can—can we learn Spanish, too?" Ginger asked.

"Certainly, you *can* because you're not stupid, Ginger. If you are asking permission to learn Spanish, the answer is the same. You certainly may. Yvonne will assist me in teaching. We shall arrange our first lesson this afternoon by learning a famous Mexican piñata song." To the freckle-faced boy she said, "I'll explain a piñata later."

Ophelia Bennett dismissed the first through third graders for recess while she talked several minutes with Yvonne, then she too went to the playground. Mrs. Bennett taught fourth through eighth graders an active game that helped them to work with fractions. After they sufficiently understood the game, Mrs. Bennett let them have their outdoor recess. She called the younger children, who had been playing tag or pushing each other on the two school swings. "Now I have a game for you that is just as much fun."

Thirty minutes later, Ophelia called everyone inside and showed the older children how to teach fractions to the younger ones.

"This kind of learning is fun! It isn't like school!" first-grader Susan said.

"Sure is fun!" Nickolas echoed.

"You must learn a new phonics game before lunch time. This is a spelling game that will help you—" She stepped to her desk and pulled open the top middle drawer. As she did, she drew back slightly. "Oh! My!" Then, pulling the drawer out farther, she reached inside and pulled out a snake. "Why, how did you find your way into my desk, you naughty little snake!" Ophelia gently rubbed the back of the reptile's head. She held the snake out toward the class and several jumped. Ginger squealed.

The boys laughed—all except Michael, the freckle-faced boy, who had gone inside during the recess period to use the boys' room. He stared at his desk.

"No need to fear this little thing, because it is the common garter snake and it is quite harmless. We shall pause now to discuss snakes for a few minutes. Observe it carefully. Most striking, of course, is that a snake has no legs. Also," and she pointed with her long, slim, index finger, "you will notice there are no eyelids, which makes the snake's eyes appear to be staring in a glassy, unblinking way. In fact, the snake's eyelid is a clear cover that protects the eye. Most snakes have only one lung; however, the python has two..."

She handed the snake to Michael and asked him to examine it and pass it on to the others. Karen feigned a squeamish noise, but none of the others said anything as each touched and passed on the garter snake.

After she spoke several minutes about snakes, Ophelia Bennett asked questions of the children and they, in turn, asked her for additional information. Most of the questions she answered. "Nickolas, please go to the encyclopedias." They were on a shelf in the back of the room. "Read the entry on snakes and discover how many varieties live in the world. Tomorrow you may give us a report. You will be the expert on reptiles."

Nickolas glowed with pride as he walked back to the encyclopedias.

"You know everything," Karen said dreamily.

With that enigmatic smile Ophelia Bennett looked at Karen. "No, my dear, not everything. But I am not afraid to ask questions and to admit what I do not know. Also, I can usually find out where to obtain the knowledge."

After the snake had been passed completely around the room, Ophelia Bennett took the reptile into her hands again. "Now, this snake obviously cannot be happy sleeping inside my desk. Hmm, what shall I do?" She walked over to the freckle-faced boy and laid the snake gently on his desk.

"I didn't—"

"Would you take care of the snake for us? Perhaps your parents might let you keep it and from time to time you could tell us of its progress."

From a startled look to a wide, toothy grin, the boy nodded vigorously as he reached out for the snake.

"Among the science supplies you will find a quart-sized jar with holes in the lid. You may keep the pet there until it is time to go home."

The freckled hand clasped the snake tightly. Forgetting he was wearing a diaper, the boy skipped to the science cupboard and put the snake inside the jar. As he sat down, he smiled at the teacher. "I like you, Mrs. Bennett. I like you a whole lot."

5

"I AM NOT CLEAR ABOUT YOUR NAME," Mrs. Bennett said. "According to my records, I find only your surname listed. Do you not have a first name?"

"No."

"What does your mother call you?"

"She's dead."

"Do you have a stepmother?"

He said nothing.

"What does she call you?"

"She just says, 'Hey, you.' "

"Your father, then? What name does he call you?"

Masters shrugged.

"Certainly he calls you by some name."

He shook his head.

"How does he address you? Does he also call out, 'Hey, you!'?"

"Sometimes."

"But he never gave you a name?"

Masters shook his head again. "Sometimes he calls me *boy*."

"What would you like to be called in this school? Since you do not have a name, perhaps we could help you to choose one."

Masters shrugged again.

"Do you like being called Boy? I had a classmate in college named Boy Greenwell. He had six older sisters and when he was born, everyone felt so happy they named him Boy."

Several students chuckled and Ginger giggled.

"Call me Boy, if you want. I don't care. I don't care at all. Masters is all right. Or Boy. Anything!" Voices whispered behind him and a flush crawled upward, beginning in his neck. "Can I—may I sit down?"

"You have a wonderful privilege, young man." Ophelia ignored his question. "This is a privilege none of us has. Take my first name: Ophelia. I hate it—I have always detested it. When I was in grade school I used to chase boys and beat them up for laughing at my name. Ophelia is the tragic heroine of Shakespeare's play, *Hamlet*, and my parents considered it a beautiful name. Many times I have wanted to change it to something simple, like Karen—"

"Ugh!" Karen bellowed, "I hate my name. It's so plain. I wish I had a name like Greta, Hedy, Claudette, or—"

"Yeah, or some other movie star name!" Nickolas laughed.

"That is precisely what I mean," Ophelia Bennett interrupted. "Most of us do not like our names. Too plain. Too difficult to spell. Something wrong with them. But Masters does not have that problem. He can call himself anything he likes; he can choose his own name."

"Tyrone is a beautiful name." Karen sighed.

"Frankenstein might be better," someone whispered.

"I—I don't care! Anything! Call me—call me Boy."

"Boy Masters? Is that what you want?" the teacher asked.

"Yes."

"All right, or would you prefer to think about it?"

"No."

"Fine, sit down, Boy." She moved from her desk to a corner of the room where an ancient piano stood. "Now, class, it is time for music. Yesterday I taught you the parts of speech and they're difficult to remember. The hardest, I have discovered, is the adverb. Here's a little song to help you understand the use of the adverb."

She sat at the piano stool, opened the piano lid, and accompanied herself:

"To find an adverb, this test try:
Ask how or when or where or why.

"Let me play it one more time and then we shall all try to sing it." She began to play again and sang in her clear alto voice, "To find an adverb..."

"Two of the keys are flat!"

Ophelia stopped playing and swiveled around on the stool. "Who said that?"

"Max said it!" the freckle-faced boy yelled as he raised his hand. "Max said it and I heard him. He's the one who said it!"

She turned toward Max. "How did you know that two of the keys were flat?"

"Because they sound that way. The second key—the one your index finger played and then after that the key you played with your little finger but had to reach for."

"Come up here and show me."

He moved quickly to the piano, tapped the D next to middle C and then the C above middle C.

"Both of them are flat. This first one is only a little off, but the other—the one you play with your little finger—that's really awful. I told Miss Perkins last year, but she only laughed at me."

"That is amazing, absolutely amazing."

Max headed back for his seat.

Ophelia Bennett went to her desk, opened the middle drawer on the right side and pawed through the contents. She extracted a pitch pipe and blew a note and then touched the C above middle C.

"See! That shows you how flat the first note is!" Then, suddenly aware of eyes on him, Max opened his geography book and pretended to read.

"Have you ever had music lessons?"

He shook his head but kept his eyes on the book.

"Talk to me after school. Anyone who has a keen ear like you have must learn music."

"Me?" His face flushed with embarrassment before he dropped his head.

"The question should be 'I?' And yes, I mean you. It would surely displease God to have you waste such an obvious talent."

He stared at her as he mumbled, "Talent?"

Facing the entire class, Ophelia Bennett announced they would return to the song, even though two keys were flat. As soon as Mrs. Bennett's fingers began to play, Max glued his gaze to the keyboard and watched every movement.

After twenty minutes, Mrs. Bennett said, "I sense you are weary of the game. We shall now sing a few popular and patriotic songs." She allowed the children to choose.

"I want to sing 'God Bless America,' " Marvin called out. "That's my favorite song."

Mrs. Bennett missed a half tone when she came to the last measure. Max winced involuntarily.

"I want to sing 'A Rainy Day in May,' " Karen called out. "We learned it last year from the other teacher."

"Hmm," Ophelia mumbled as she tapped out several notes on the piano, trying to find where to start. "I am not certain...." She bent her head down and tried several notes, none of which seemed quite right. Before she realized what was happening, Max stood beside her. He reached past her right hand and struck the D flat minor chord. "That's where it starts, Mrs. Bennett."

"How did you know that?"

"I watched Miss Perkins's hands while she played. She doesn't play the left hand very well and she beats everything like it's marching music, but I watched her fingers. Every time she played, she started at the same place, only she had the music sheet."

"Stand here and watch me," Ophelia instructed and began to play the requested song. In the middle of the chorus she stopped and fingered several keys trying to find the correct note.

"This one, Mrs. Bennett," he said quietly as he tapped the D flat key.

"You have been my teacher this morning. What a marvelous gift God has given you! Thank you so much. I can hardly wait for you to learn to play so I can sit back and sing with the students. You *will* be able to do that, you know."

Max walked back to his seat, but he didn't bury his face this time. He looked at Mrs. Bennett as she announced the final song, "Columbia, the Gem of the Ocean."

"How did you do that? Those notes all sound the same to me," Nickolas said to Max.

"Yeah, I know. I've heard you sing."

Nickolas laughed heartily and slapped Max good-naturedly across the shoulder. Even Karen glanced at Max with a different light in her eyes.

*

At lunchtime, Nickolas invited Boy and Max to play catch with him. They declined, but Nickolas persisted. "Look, it's easy."

"Easy for you," Max said, dismissing Nickolas.

"I guess so. Like music for you," Nickolas conceded and waved as he called out for anyone to join him in a game of catch.

Max and Boy looked at each other and then both of them smiled.

6

FRIDAY OF THE FIRST WEEK OF SCHOOL had been the first day at North Prairie that Boy had ever liked. After lunch, Mrs. Bennett chose him as captain on the phonics team to help the primary grades.

At 2:30, Boy's triumphant day crashed. Along with Yvonne and the two third graders, Larry and Carol Kent, he worked at the art table where they prepared a drawing to illustrate life in medieval times. Using a history book as a guide, Boy had already sketched a castle in the background, a field of grain in the foreground, and a mendicant monk in the foreground. At his corner of the table he deftly blended colored chalks and crayon.

"That's swell. Just swell," Larry said. "Wish I could draw." He looked down at his initial efforts that consisted mostly of gray and black wiggly lines, which was his attempt of creating a knight in armor.

"It's nothing."

"It is, too!" Larry insisted.

"Mrs. Bennett! Mrs. Bennett! Look at this! It's beautiful!" Yvonne snatched Boy's paper and held it up for the teacher, who sat with the science group.

"Give that back to me!" Boy lurched forward to retrieve the manila drawing paper but reached too far and fell clumsily against the edge of the table. Twisting, he sprawled on to the floor where he landed on his back. When he fell, a sharp pain raced through his leg, which was twisted under his body. Even worse, when he started to move, he heard the rip of the seam of his bib overalls—right at the buttocks.

He lay on the floor several seconds trying to figure out what to do. If he got up, all the children would see what had happened—and Boy felt doubly embarrassed because he had no underwear. Almost immediately several classmates had crowded around him. He couldn't just lie there.

"Lemme alone," he growled. "I'm okay; just lemme alone for a minute."

As they backed away, a sudden inspiration grabbed hold of Boy. He lay on his back, less than ten feet from the boys' lavatory. He sat up and began to scoot himself across the floor and toward the boys' room. He pushed the door open and backed inside. He would remain there until school ended and the others had gone.

Minutes later, Boy heard a gentle tap on the door. "Yeah?"

"Are you all right?" Mrs. Bennett asked.

"Yes…I'm…just a little sick at my stomach, I guess."

She walked away and he heard her organizing the remaining thirty-two students for a spelling game.

*

A pair of deep-brown eyes glared at Ophelia Bennett as she opened the door of the North Prairie School.

"I want to talk to you! Right now!"

She gave the stranger a brief nod before she called back into the classroom, "All right, children, you are dismissed. I shall see each of you Monday morning." She held the door open for them to leave.

"Now! I want to talk to you right now!" Although more than six feet tall, the visitor gave the impression of broadness. His wide face and massive hands strengthened that initial impression. His muscular arms reminded Ophelia of a picture in the fourth-grade reader depicting Longfellow's village blacksmith.

"Certainly, just as soon as I have dismissed all of the children. If you will be good enough to move away—you are blocking the door."

He stepped back and the children filed past. She had a word or a smile for every student. Nickolas, usually near the front of the line, lingered at the rear. She looked at the man again. Despite his years and broader features, the resemblance was obvious.

When Nickolas approached, he stammered, "Mrs. Bennett, I didn't mean...honest I didn't intend to—to get you into trouble—"

"I certainly understand," she said. "You need not concern yourself." She patted his shoulder and smiled.

The boy dashed past her as he mumbled, "Hello, Dad."

"I'll talk to you later, son. Go on home now. This matter concerns the teacher 'n' me," he replied gruffly.

"Then please come in and we shall talk, Mr. Harrison. I'm Mrs. Benn—"

"I know who you are, and you'll learn pretty quick just who I am! I come to straighten out a few things around here."

"Do come in."

After she stepped backward to allow Mr. Harrison to precede her into the classroom, Ophelia Bennett gave one final glance to the schoolyard and called out, "Good-bye, boys and girls! We shall have an even better class Monday!"

The cheeriness of her voice relieved the anxiety of Nickolas and the others who lingered outside the school. They slowly wandered off in different directions.

After she closed the door, Ophelia Bennett walked briskly to her desk. Mr. Harrison had pulled up the only other chair and sat stiffly waiting for her.

"Is there something I am able to do for—"

"You know why I'm here! You got no right keeping my Nickolas until nearly six o'clock the first day of school and making him clean every one of them blasted, dirty desks. That's why we got a janitor. I'm here to straighten you out and to warn you—"

"One minute, Mr. Harrison! You do not burst into this school and you do not shout and threaten me. If you will calm down and speak to me as one human being speaks to another, I shall be pleased to listen. But I will not tolerate this bullish behavior!"

"Bullish behavior? Just a minute! Who d'you think—"

"I refuse to attempt conversation with anyone who cannot control his temper. Your enormous size in no way intimidates me. The world is filled with monstrous people who think that size and force qualify them to rule over weaker and smaller people. If that reflects your attitude, you are quite wrong, Mr. Harrison. Quite wrong."

She picked up a pencil and began grading papers, ignoring him. After several more seconds, adding as though it were an afterthought, she said, "When you are ready to treat me as a human being, please begin. Until then I shall not speak another word to you."

"Who in the—" He pounded loudly on her desk. "Just hold on one minute there!"

Ophelia Bennett continued grading papers. "Hmmm, I shall have to work with the third graders on capitalization." She jotted down a note on a large day-by-day planning calendar in the center of her desk.

"Don't hand me that, lady! I won't stand for it!"

The redheaded teacher continued grading papers. She hummed Gershwin's "Summertime."

He shouted again and blasted an assortment of four-letter words, but Ophelia Bennett gave no indication that she had heard him. After she had corrected all the papers, she carefully recorded the grades in her book.

Mr. Harrison pounded the desk again and his eyes bore into the teacher's skull. She did not flinch. After she had entered the grades in the book, she closed it, laid it aside, and carefully straightened up her desk. She took her purse from an inner recess of the desk and pushed her chair against the desk. She walked past Mr. Harrison as though he did not exist and headed for the door.

"Mrs. Bennett, please—"

"Yes, Mr. Harrison, you wish to speak to me?" She turned slightly.

"I got mad because Nickolas didn't get home Tuesday until six o'clock. Said he'd been here scrubbing up these dang—I mean, those dirty desks in the school."

"That is correct."

"I don't like that."

"I am delighted to hear you say those words. I did not enjoy watching your son mutilate property that does not belong to him. Did he tell you why I kept him?"

"Sure. But marking on *one* desk? I mean—"

"How many desks should he have marred before I punished him?"

"It—it just don't seem right. I mean, washing all them desks because he did a little marking on *one* desk."

"Please look at the desks in this classroom. Look at the markings, carvings, gouges, and mutilations!"

"Yes'm. That's what I mean. They're all marked up and—"

"Allow me to explain something to you. North Prairie holds the unique reputation as the most badly disciplined school in Lake County and perhaps in the entire state of Illinois. I intend to change that. To accomplish that goal, I need Nickolas's help. Obviously, your son has great leadership qualities. I hope you are proud of him. Are you? Are you proud of your son?"

"I...I am, of course, uh, I mean..."

"Do not say 'of course.' He has outstanding leadership qualities. However, a leader without discipline and without consideration for others is no true leader. Would you agree with that?"

"Yeah, I guess so."

"Nickolas is large physically and quite good looking. Every girl fawns over him, and he is a remarkable young man. But I do not want him to become satisfied with getting by because he is handsome. He can become a good athlete and he has the personality that will enable him to get along quite well with people—"

"Uh, thank you—"

"However, I see deeper qualities in your son. He has leadership ability, and I want to mold him into being not merely a leader—he does not need my influence for that, but more than that. I will never be satisfied until he also exhibits qualities of kindness, consideration, and compassion." She eyed Nickolas's father. "And he can be a leader, you see. He has such vast potential."

"I never thought about it like—"

"I punished him severely for a single act of defacement. He respects me for having done that. And because of his attitude, I am already immensely proud of your son. He took his punishment like a gentleman. I cannot believe he went home and complained to you."

"Complain? That's part of what made me so mad. It took me more'n twenty minutes to drag the story out of him. And you know what made me the maddest? He kept saying, 'I deserved it.' And that was too much! No teacher before has ever punished my Nickolas like—"

"Which is most unfortunate. But you need not worry. It is not too late for him yet."

"That's not what I meant."

"I know what you meant. I hope you realize what I mean."

"You're tough, ain't you? Yeah, I can see why Nickolas likes you. You ain't afraid, neither."

Ophelia Bennett smiled and murmured, "Long ago, I learned that when I do what is right, I have nothing—and no one—to fear."

Harrison opened his mouth, shut it, and then shuffled his feet for a full minute. "Uh, ma'am, I guess I sounded kinda mean when I done come in here."

"That was twenty minutes ago. We are long past that now, are we not? I have great dreams for Nickolas. He can make you wonderfully proud of him. But he has lessons he must learn before he can realize that potential. I assure you that by the end of this school year, you will be pleased that I have disciplined him."

"I hope so." Then he grinned, and she realized where Nickolas had inherited that winning face that seemed so boyish and warm. "I mean, yeah, guess you're right."

Just then Mrs. Bennett jerked her head to the side in time to see the door to the boys' lavatory close. "Oh," she said, and her hand went up to her mouth, "forgive me. I forgot."

Mr. Harrison looked puzzled.

"One of the other boys had an—an accident. He was not feeling well and he stayed in the boys' lavatory. I must take him home immediately. Please excuse me."

"Yeah, sure." Mr. Harrison got out of his chair, extended his massive hand, and shook the teacher's long, slim fingers. Without another word, he walked out of the classroom.

*

Ophelia Bennett tapped on the boys' lavatory door. "Boy. Boy, can you come out?"

Seconds later, the door opened and Boy walked out and faced her.

"How do you feel?"

"I'm okay now."

"Your stomach is all right?"

"Yes'm."

"I shall take you home."

"Aw, it's not...," he said slowly, yet he hoped she would. He had been trying to picture how he could walk the two miles with the gaping tear in his overalls.

"I could do nothing less. Are you certain you are feeling all right? Would you like me to take you to a doctor?"

"Yes'm, I'm fine. Not sick or nothin'—I mean, anything. Honest."

Boy insisted on locking the school door and carrying her small satchel of papers as he followed her out to her Ford. He opened the door for her to get seated and closed the door before he went around to the other side.

"Thank you," she said.

He smiled to himself as he realized no one would see him as he made his way home.

During the drive, Mrs. Bennett chatted with Boy and asked him questions about his father, learned that his mother had been dead since he was four years old, and that he dearly loved his aunt, who lived next door and took care of him.

As soon as they arrived at the Masters's farm, he pointed out the driveway, which led to a small frame building nearly hidden by three large maple trees. "This is just fine, and I thank you." He pulled down the handle to open the door. "I'll jump out here at the road, ma'am. You don't need to go up the driveway."

"I think I ought to drive you—"

"No, ma'am. This is fine." He jumped out of the car.

Ophelia Bennett stopped and kept her foot on the brake pedal.

When Boy got out of the car, he completely forgot why he had ridden home with Mrs. Bennett. He had run at least twenty-five feet before he turned to wave a final good-bye. She waved back.

Just then he remembered. Boy faced her car as she drove away. He wondered if she had seen the cause of his embarrassment.

7

"MAX, PLAYING OUTSIDE IS AS IMPORTANT AS STUDYING INSIDE. You need both. I want you and Larry to go out on the playground with the others."

"Aw, Mrs. Bennett, this is fun. I'd rather stay in here, and besides—"

"Yeah, me, too!" third-grader Larry interrupted. "I never knew school could be fun before. 'Course we didn't have this kinda school before, either."

"It's almost like not learning." Max stared out the window. "I mean, there's so much I want to know about what's in these books. And I'm not afraid to ask questions—not anymore—and I'm not afraid to ask you to explain when I still don't understand."

"Yeah, me too," Larry said.

"That is the best way to learn, boys," she said as she closed Larry's copy of *Call of the Wild.* "Because you want to. It is not only pleasurable but the kind of learning that belongs to you. No one can ever take it away, and you do not learn it merely to prepare for a test."

"Yeah, so can I—I mean, may I—stay inside a little longer and—"

She swatted Larry lightly and he jumped from his desk and ran toward the door.

Max had not moved. "Uh, then, uh, maybe I ought to stay inside and learn a lot more, don't you think?" he asked with only the slightest trace of a smile.

"No, I think you need to go outside and exercise. When you come back, your mind will be refreshed and you will feel even more eager to study again. Even fun becomes dull if that is all you ever do."

"Okay, Mrs. Bennett," he replied in a dejected tone before his face broke into a broad grin.

"I want you to build a strong body to match that good mind."

The boy flushed. He hopped from his desk and headed toward the door. He heard her call after him, "I believe in you, Max!"

"Why?" he asked and turned around.

"Because I do. That is not an answerable question. Or perhaps it is that I can see things in you that others have not yet seen. God has given me that ability—to see good qualities in people like you—the kind of qualities that often get overlooked."

"Nobody ever treated me the way you do. They just called me dumb."

"People sometimes do or say unkind things. They do not always realize how cruel their remarks sound. But you are not stupid. You have a quick mind."

He nodded and opened the door. Then he stopped. "Mrs. Bennett, I broke the second rule this morning, didn't I? Concentration. The sixth graders were having so much fun with their geography game that I listened to them instead of studying. But I'll keep trying. Honest."

"Of course you will. The important thing is not to doubt yourself." She walked toward him and patted him gently on the shoulder. "I do not doubt you. Keep telling yourself that. Keep saying, 'I can do it.' "

"Yeah, but I'm not so good at that. I mean, I never had no—I mean *any*—practice doing that."

"Yes, I understand." From her pocket she pulled out a postcard-sized piece of paper. "This is something I wish you to read and say every day until you believe it."

Max walked back to her and took the paper from her hand. Silently, he read the words.

"It is a verse from the Bible." She quoted Philippians 4:13: "I can do all things through Christ which strengtheneth me."

"Uh, well, I'll read it and—"

"Read it many times. Every day. To be effective, that verse must become part of you." She moved closer to him and Max could smell the faintest fragrance of lilac. "This verse is a special message for you. It is one that I want you to remember the rest of your life."

"I'll learn it. I promise."

After Max left the classroom, Ophelia sat at her desk and took out her folder marked *Students.* Under the page labeled *Max Waxman,* she wrote in her precise Palmer-style penmanship:

> Max evidences an unusual quickness. Apparently now that his vision has been corrected with glasses, along with adequate attention that encourages his learning, this student has made remarkable improvement. More than any other student in the classroom, he can work alone with only occasional directions. Note: He still needs frequent encouragement.

*

In the middle of the afternoon, after the students had completed a nature study by examining and identifying four different species of butterflies, Marvin said, "You know, Mrs. Bennett, I've learned a lot since you came here."

"I am pleased that you have and I agree that you have progressed well. You are an extremely intelligent young man."

"But why didn't the other teachers do things like this?" Boy asked.

"That is difficult to state simply. Trying anything new frightens some people. Or they seem to think that the only way to learn is to sit quietly at your desk and memorize facts and information."

"I hate that," a voice from the back said.

"At times such methods are beneficial. I choose, however, to use a variety of methods so that you will enjoy learning and—"

"I hope it will always be like this," Karen breathed dramatically.

"Private schools have experimented and tried these ideas for years. There are a few of us teachers who want to introduce learning by fun methods into public education."

"But you know, I think there's something else—you make it fun for us. But you really like us, don't you?"

*

Ginger, constructing a piñata out of papier-mâché, heard the approaching car first. She ran to the teacher's desk and whispered in Mrs. Bennett's ear.

"Thank you."

The frown on Ginger's face changed to a smile. "We used to do that for the other teachers so they wouldn't get caught shouting at us."

"Yes, I understand. Now please go back to your work." The teacher nodded and continued her penmanship with the first graders. The fifth and sixth graders, who had written a play about General George Washington, rehearsed in one corner. Seventh and eighth graders were preparing for a program on Mexico, all except for Yvonne, who was teaching Max the words of a Mexican folksong, and he was teaching her to sing harmony.

Exactly three minutes later, the door opened—not merely opened but banged against the wall. Karen whispered to Catherine, "It's like a famous actress making her entry to the stage."

Marvin turned automatically and muttered, "Ye gads and little fishes."

Nickolas made faces at those sitting near him.

The figure stood inside the room and surveyed the activities. No one stopped working, even though the fifth graders stole furtive glances. Several did not even turn around, but they too knew who had come in. The second and third graders seemed to work harder at the language table as they prepared their spelling lesson.

Without her shoes, the woman would have been exactly five feet tall. What she lacked in height she compensated for in weight, with a large ring of fat bulging around the waist of her plain blue cotton dress, despite the restrictions of her tightly fitted corset. She wore the slightest trace of lipstick and must have spent extra minutes that morning carefully working in rouge so she would appear healthy-cheeked. Her brown hair was piled in a high pompadour, fashioned much like Bette Davis's in one of her recent films. The brown eyes, too small for her wide face, squinted as she scrutinized the room.

Her mouth dropped open and she stood, one hand extended, the other hanging limply at her side. "Ohhhh."

No one acknowledged her presence. Even Mrs. Bennett seemed not to know that Miss Perkins had returned to North Prairie School.

"But—you're—you're studying—working—all of you!" she squealed. Then, as if on a signal, thirty-four heads turned almost in unison and stared.

The newcomer advanced three steps so she was now clearly visible to Ophelia Bennett. She breathed deeply and yelled, "Good morning! I'm Edwina Perkins! I teach fifth through eighth grades!" Her nervousness showed by her high-pitched tones.

"Yes, of course. Please come in, Miss Perkins," the redheaded teacher called. She leaned toward her first graders and said, "Finish the page just as I showed you." She left her desk and walked across the room to where Miss Perkins stood.

The younger teacher shifted her gaze from pupil to pupil, as if unable to grasp what she was seeing. "What—what is going on?"

"I am Ophelia Bennett. As Mr. Pettygill has probably informed you, I have been teaching all the students for the two weeks you have been ill." She extended her hand. "Welcome back to North Prairie."

"Yes—yes, uh, thank you." She shook the older woman's hand lightly and stared around the room, taking in the disarray of desks as well as children whispering, even talking out loud with each other. "I'm certain you're glad to have me back to take some of these ruffians off your hands!" the brittle voice barked as Miss Perkins started moving around the room. "Imagine they've been giving you fits!"

"No, not in the least," Ophelia Bennett replied. "They have been extremely well behaved. I have had absolutely no trouble."

"I'm glad for that!" Edwina said as she reached Ophelia's desk. She lowered her voice only slightly. "I sent word that I'd beat the tar out of them if they gave you any trouble. I'm glad they took me at my word."

"They have cooperated extremely well," Ophelia said, the tiny lines at the corner of her mouth revealing the marks of a smile.

"You and I can get acquainted later, I'm sure." Edwina Perkins turned abruptly and faced the students, all of whom appeared absorbed in their activities. "All right, up now! All of you from fifth to eighth grades! Let's put away all the drawing paper and clutter and we'll go to our own room!"

No one moved, as though none of them had heard her loud voice. Furtive glances flicked from face to face.

"No dawdling!" she commanded.

The voice sounded more like that of an army sergeant rather than a drab woman in her early twenties.

Edwina pulled at Nickolas's collar but he said calmly, "Thank you, Miss Perkins, but I'd like to stay in Mrs. Bennett's room this year."

"I should say not! I know your tricks, Nickolas! You would drive that poor Mrs. Bennett crazy! Quickly now, no more of your wasting time!"

Nickolas slowly moved from his desk, then reached over and punched Max, who now wore glasses. "You, too, Max." And then, under his breath, "Sorry."

Max didn't move. As if he had no realization of what went on around him, he continued writing about the Aztecs of Mexico. Several of the older students turned and looked pleadingly into the face of Ophelia Bennett. She nodded as if to say, "Do as she asks" and returned to her desk.

"Max! *Now!*" screamed Miss Perkins as she stood at the door and the others filed by. "Thank you, Mrs. Bennett, for putting up with such badly behaved—"

"As I said, they behaved extremely well. They are fine students—all of them."

"Uh, yes, of course, even if they get out of hand now and then."

Max looked up at Mrs. Bennett and with his lips said noiselessly, "Please."

Ophelia Bennett blinked and turned her attention toward the first graders.

"Do I have to go?" Max asked Mrs. Bennett.

"I should say so!" screamed Miss Perkins. "How dare you torment her one more second! You have to go and you have to go now!"

"But you promised!" He made no effort to move and his eyes stayed on Mrs. Bennett's face. "This is the beginning of the third week—"

"Now!" commanded Miss Perkins.

Mrs. Bennett remained motionless and expressionless. Max dropped his gaze, threw his books angrily on top of each other, and stomped toward the door.

Mrs. Bennett rose from behind her desk and walked rapidly down the aisle. In a whisper she said, "Max, it will be all right. I promise you." Her intense gaze seemed to send a second message into his clouded, hazel eyes. Even though she did not say anything more, he calmed, as if he could feel her voice in his head saying, "Did I not promise you, Max? I am going to help you. Everything will be all right, just as I promised."

He smiled at Ophelia Bennett and said in a low voice, "Okay, I'll try."

Boy had still made no effort to move, allowing only his gaze to follow Mrs. Bennett.

"Masters! You heard me! Don't play deaf!"

He glared at Miss Perkins for several seconds before he turned his head back to a Spanish grammar book he had opened.

"I will not take this insolence from you, young man! Up! March into that room before I lose my temper!"

Boy slammed the book closed but still made no effort to move. "Please," he whispered to Mrs. Bennett, "please help us." When she said nothing, his dark eyes concentrated on her face and pleaded silently for deliverance from the overpowering force.

Mrs. Bennett simply said, "Boy will go with you now."

"Boy?" the squat teacher asked. "His name is Masters. Just Masters, nothing else."

"Yes, I know that was his name last year. He has now chosen Boy as his first name. We have agreed to respect his wishes."

"Hmph!" snorted the teacher as she headed toward his desk.

Boy made one final, nonverbal appeal to Mrs. Bennett. Her only response was a slight nod.

"Yeah, I—I guess I understand," he said softly. "You can't do anything, can you?"

"Not yet," she murmured. "Be patient."

Boy surprised her with a full grin before he turned back to Miss Perkins. He regarded her with what appeared to be a forced smile. "I'm sorry for not coming right away," he said. "I'm coming right now." The smile died on his face. One at a time, he picked up his four books and started toward the other classroom. "Thank you for all your splendid help, Mrs. Bennett," he said aloud without turning around.

"That's better, much better." Edwina Perkins waddled into her room, trailed by Max and Boy.

*

As soon as they were gone, Ophelia Bennett walked over to the chalkboard and tried to focus on her twenty remaining students. Although not certain how the events would transpire, she had already sensed the outcome.

She held up the third-grade reader and told them to turn to page 34. "Today, we are going to learn about the silent letters in words." She wrote *glisten* and *listen* on the board. "The letter T is silent in both words. Now pronounce both words properly."

She waited for them to read both words. "On page 34 are nine more words with silent letters. You must find them, write them down, and then we shall see how well you did."

Every child opened a third-grade reader, even the first and second graders.

Less than a minute later, Edwina Perkins stalked into the classroom. "There you are! Yvonne, you naughty thing! You belong in my class! You know you do! Last year you were in the fourth grade and I passed you because you're too old to stay with the younger children!"

The girl's eyes remained focused on her book. She had already discovered four of the words.

"Yvonne! You come—"

Then, as though suddenly aware of the concentration of the children, Miss Perkins stopped. Her face flushed and she covered it up by putting her hand to her mouth and coughing lightly. She walked over to the chalkboard and sighed. "I'm sorry for intruding like this. Yvonne belongs in my class and I'm sure you'll be glad to get rid of her. She's such a hopeless child. But that's part of the burden of our profession, isn't it?"

"I would not say—"

"Yvonne! Now! Move!"

The small, dark-haired girl stared defiantly back at her teacher.

When the Mexican girl made no attempt to leave her desk, Miss Perkins yelled, "Yvonne! I called you to go into my classroom! Now! Move!"

Slowly the child turned her face toward Miss Perkins. With a blank expression she said coldly, *"No comprende, Senorita."*

"Why, you little smart aleck! How dare you—"

"No comprende, Senorita."

In a movement surprisingly rapid for a woman of her size, Miss Perkins raced to Yvonne's desk and snatched one of her pigtails. She yanked it several times as the girl yelped in pain.

"No! No!" screamed Yvonne, although she left her desk and followed Miss Perkins toward the back of the room. *"Tu eres una vieja vaca!"* (You are an old cow!)

"Yvonne, please go with her quietly and respectfully," Mrs. Bennett said.

"Solamente porque tù lo decis, lo harè." (Only because you say so, I will do it.)

When the door closed behind Yvonne and Miss Perkins, Ophelia Bennett walked casually among her remaining students as if there had been no interruption. "You are doing well. Most of you have already found four or five words with silent letters. Yes, and I see that Michael has seven already. Very good."

"Isn't it going to be awful lonesome in here?" the boy with the perpetual questions asked.

"Isn't there any way we can get them back? I could trip Miss Perkins and maybe she'd break her leg. Or I could let all the air out of her tires," suggested James Watkins of the second grade. "That's what my brother did when he was in school."

Mrs. Bennett laughed. "I understand your anger and your disappointment—"

"But it still isn't fair!" Michael said.

"This is correct. And one of the great lessons you must learn is that life is not always fair. You must make the best of what you have, even if bad things seem stronger than good, and even in your greatest disappointments."

"Can't you do something?" Michael asked. "I didn't like you or any of the other kids at first, but now we're...well, we're kinda friends like and—"

"No, there is nothing to be done at the moment. I am still here with you. We will have many, many more days together. When I am gone—" For a moment a cloud spread across the face of Ophelia Bennett, but she banished it almost as quickly as it had appeared. "But for now, I ask you not to worry."

"Yes, but when?" Gerald Jenkins blurted out. "Oh, I'm sorry. I didn't raise my hand, did I?"

She smiled and patted the top of his unruly brown hair. Standing in front of her desk, she leaned back against it slightly. "This is now our third week of school. I promised you that, after two weeks together, you could vote whether you wanted to continue the way I teach or return to your old ways."

"I like school the way you teach. I didn't expect to learn anything and now I really want to learn everything," Michael, the outspoken first grader, said. "And I don't want to vote. I just want to keep doing it like you've been doing it with us."

"Me, too," James said. "This is fun!"

Stephen Lawson from the second grade raised his hand. "Mrs. Bennett, until you came, I hated school and sometimes I begged my daddy not to make me come here. If we go back to the same dumb way of learning things I'll hate it again."

"Yeah," Gerald said. "It wasn't really any fun letting air out of tires and stealing the toilet paper. We only did it because—" he looked at his feet a minute—"because, oh, I don't know why. Maybe because we hated school so much. But now we're having fun and this is the way it ought to be."

"So please don't stop," third grader Carol begged.

Each of the twenty remaining children either spoke up or vigorously nodded. After she had given everyone a chance to speak, Ophelia Bennett said, "We shall continue our way of doing things. We must finish the game of the silent letters first. And then we shall start our history lesson this morning. Instead of learning only a lot of facts about what happened in the past, we are going to live in the past. You will become the people we study. I shall give you recipes to take home. With your parents' help, we shall cook and eat the same type of food they did."

The children read and re-read page 34, searching for all nine words. A robin perched on the windowsill. Even though separated by glass, its trill filled the room. Chugging vibrations from a passing tractor momentarily distracted some of them.

"I've got eight now." Susan, a bright first grader, smiled. "This is the best I've ever, ever done in school."

The door separating both classrooms opened quietly and Ginger closed it behind her. "Uh, Mrs. Bennett, I forgot my pencil. I must have left it in my desk." She lingered a long time and finally fished a pencil out of her dress pocket. "I found it!" she said and left.

For the next half hour, the thirteen students from Miss Perkins's class came into the room. They had to use the lavatory, needed paper, or had forgotten a book. Ophelia Bennett continued to teach as if she scarcely noticed the interruptions.

Carol was the first to find the ninth word with a silent letter—the K in doorknob.

After checking to make certain the children had written all nine on their papers, Mrs. Bennett then moved on to teaching the history lesson, which began with the settlement of the New World by Europeans.

As Mrs. Bennett walked around the room, the excitement grew in her voice and the children's faces shone. She explained how they were to work in groups of five and gave them each a specific nation to study. "Now, you must work on your own. I shall walk around to see how you are doing. I will give you hints if you get confused or do not understand, but you must try to figure out your assignments yourself."

As the children scurried around the room, Ginger walked in a second time, "Sorry, but this time I got permission to use the lavatory." She ducked her head for a minute. "But that's not the reason."

"To lie is not—"

Ginger's eyes now focused on Ophelia Bennett. "I know that was wrong, but I had to get out of there for a minute. You see, we all voted in the other room. Every one of us agreed that we want to study your way. Nickolas sent a note around and we all signed our names." She handed the sheet of ruled paper to the teacher. "Now it's up to you to get us out of that—that dungeon!" She walked rapidly back toward her classroom. With her hand on the doorknob, she swiveled. Wiping misty eyes, she said in a throaty voice, "Please. Please help us."

Minutes later Nickolas walked into Ophelia's classroom. "Uh, I gave all my notebook paper to Stephen." As Stephen Lawson handed Nickolas several sheets of paper, the upper-class student said, "Mrs. Bennett, we're counting on you! You can't let us down."

Every five minutes—exactly—one of the students came from Miss Perkins's room. They borrowed books, pencils, or erasers, or went to the lavatory. By 10:30, the normal recess period, the younger children headed for the playground.

Ophelia Bennett heard the screeching voice of Edwina Perkins: "No! You will have no recess period today! You've all been to the lavatory at least twice this morning! That's enough! You will each sit down and do your work! Max! Max! Do your work! Max, are you deaf? Don't you hear me?"

Ophelia Bennett leaned against the side wall and closed her eyes. Max had made remarkable progress in the two weeks she had helped him. Although he worked quickly, his span of concentration had been limited. By watching him carefully, keeping him absorbed, and offering new challenges he could meet, his progress had been extremely good. He had gone from the primer reading stage to a third-grade level. His spelling equaled an average third grader. He was still weak in arithmetic. She'd have to devise a new series of games to challenge him in that area. She decided she would have to talk to him after school.

"Don't you yell at me again!" a boy's voice said angrily.

"I'm your teacher! I'll yell anytime I want! And if you'd listen and do what I say, I wouldn't have to yell!"

"And if you could teach, you wouldn't need to yell all the time!"

Ophelia Bennett awakened from her mind wandering. The words had come through the door clearly but muffled enough that it took her a moment to realize that Max had screamed. *Max?* In the two weeks, no matter how provoked the boy had been, she had never heard him raise his voice. Max?

"Just sit down and do what I assigned you!"

"I won't and you can't make me!"

The boy charged into Ophelia Bennett's classroom with Miss Perkins right behind him. She grabbed the boy by the back of his belt and pulled him toward herself. He stopped suddenly and jerked around, unintentionally striking her across the face. Then he pushed her backward. "Don't you ever touch me again as long as you live! Not ever! Do you hear me?"

Miss Perkins sank to the floor as Max ran through the school and outside. Ophelia Bennett knelt beside her. "I'm sorry, Edwina. He did not intend to hurt you." She helped the shorter woman to her feet.

Edwina rubbed her face as if in a daze. "That isn't like Max. Why, I've taught him for two years and he's never so much as sassed back once. He's never been mean before. What's gotten into him? He is a little on the stupid side, but this—"

"Max is not stupid. I regret what just happened to you and it does not excuse his behavior, but Max *is not* stupid. Please, don't speak that way about him. Max is not even average. Max is highly intelligent."

"I was speaking of his performance for the past—"

"I am speaking about the real Max—the brilliant youngster who is barely beginning to move forward in his development."

"Well, I never!"

"I am not trying to offend you."

The squinting brown eyes peered at Ophelia Bennett, then scanned the room. Pulling herself together, she declared, "I don't know what's gotten into those children. They're *impossible.* We haven't accomplished one objective today. As soon as I say a single sentence—even the simplest thing—I get all kinds of questions or someone wants to leave the room. I tried to stop them and Nickolas stood and said, 'If I don't get to the lavatory now, I'll wet my pants and my dad will be mad at somebody.' Then he dashed out. Why, I've never seen the class like this before." Edwina Perkins rubbed her face, patted down her corset, and straightened the waist on her blue dress. “To begin with, they’re terrible children to teach—all of them! Terrible! But this year, they’re worse—worse than they’ve ever been.”

“Children! Please go out to the playground and remain outside for recess!” Ophelia called to the upper-class children who had gathered at the door, watching silently. “Miss Perkins and I are having a brief teachers’ meeting.”

“You promised,” called Ginger, moving toward the door.

“Everything is under control.” Ophelia’s calm voice belied the command written on her face.

“I’m counting on you,” Nickolas said, turned toward the others. “Okay, everyone, let’s go. You heard Mrs. Bennett.” As if commanded by a platoon sergeant, they lined up two abreast and marched outside. Not one of them lingered.

Ophelia smiled to herself. They were outside where neither teacher could see them, but she knew they would hear every word spoken inside the classroom.

“These past two weeks must have been horrible for you,” Miss Perkins said. “Absolutely horrible, I’m sure.”

“On the contrary, we have had an excellent two weeks.”

“Don’t tell me that—” But one look at Ophelia Bennett must have convinced Edwina Perkins that the redheaded teacher had spoken the truth. “What did you do? I mean, how did you handle them?”

“I have a few methods. But most of all, my dear, I loved them.”

“I love them too, but they still drive me nearly crazy. You saw what—”

“Love will lead where force can’t drive.”

8

OPHELIA BENNETT RANG THE SCHOOL BELL AT 3:30. The younger children, as if alerted to remain in their seats, did nothing. Seconds later, the upper-class students stopped en masse at her desk.

"Please, please, you must help us," Karen pleaded, quoting and emoting in her best Joan Crawford mode, "I have no idea how much more of this—this tyrannical oppression I can bear."

"We voted again after lunch," Nickolas said, "and Ginger lost, so she's in there talking to Miss Perkins until we finish here."

Despite her resolve not to, Ophelia Bennett smiled and then shook her head slowly. "You are only confirming that you are quite an intelligent group of students. And, I now add, extremely resourceful."

"That's 'cause you've helped us," Boy said quietly. "Now we ain't—aren't—afraid."

"And we know what we want," Yvonne said. "This is—this has been the time of my life. Never have I been as happy as I have been in your class."

"So, see, you have to help us," Nickolas said. "Not just Yvonne. That's all of us. We hated school before, so you can't let us down now."

"Oh, yes, you must. You really, really must help us," Karen said in her best imitation of Katharine Hepburn.

Mrs. Bennett gazed into their faces as they continued to complain about the horrible treatment and their desire to return to the one classroom setting.

"And Max—what about Max?" Boy asked. "He's my friend, and Miss Perkins, well, she probably won't let him come back and...and he didn't mean to hurt her. He said so, and Max wouldn't lie."

"Tell him to return tomorrow, will you? I think it will all be worked out by then."

"It had better be. That fat, old cow—" Nickolas said.

"Stop that kind of talk, young man! I will not allow you to talk that way against anyone, and especially not against your teacher. Do you understand?"

"I'm sorry, but she's so—"

"At the moment you are angry. I understand your wish to speak harshly, but that does not make it acceptable. Part of growing up means that you not only learn information, but you also learn to control such anger. At the moment you do not like her."

"Not like her?" Yvonne said. "I detest that—"

"No! None of that. Even if you do not like her, you may not insult her. Is that clear?"

The children either nodded or dropped their gaze.

"You must respect her. Even if you do not like her methods, you will show her respect, just as you would any other person."

"Yes, ma'am," Boy said.

"She truly cares for you. She is doing her best."

"If that's her best," Boy said, then added, "all right, I know it is. I don't like her very much, but, I guess she's doing the best she knows how."

"We haven't been very good students, have we?" Marvin asked. "I mean, we haven't given her a chance."

"I just got mad," Nickolas said, "and then when she talked that way to Max, why—"

"You have a kind heart, Nickolas, and that is commendable. But a truly kind heart is generous to *everyone*—even to one's enemies." She patted his shoulder. "So let us understand this much. Under no conditions will I allow you to speak against her or anyone with vile or abusive words."

"Then what shall we do?" Karen asked, giving her best imitation of Greta Garbo. "We cannot go on this way."

"I am not sure...not yet. But I know everything will be better tomorrow. Go home now. I shall speak with Miss Perkins."

"We won't stay in there," Marvin said.

Nickolas put his arm on Marvin's shoulder. "She's right. Aw, okay, Mrs. Bennett, we'll do what you say. But remember, we voted to keep on with your kind of teaching."

"Thank you."

"We'll burn down her room if we have to."

"You have such fire in your veins. I hope that before you go into high school next year, we can control that temper. You have so much to offer in leadership if you can first lead yourself."

He nodded slowly. "Yes, ma'am." Then his face beamed. "You're the first person who has ever made me want to be better."

"Oh, yes, yes," Karen said. "I feel the same way."

"C'mon, then," Nickolas said and the others followed him out of the room.

"Bye, Mrs. Bennett," Catherine said and waved.

"Buenos noches," Yvonne called out.

Boy laughed. *"Hasta luego."*

Mrs. Bennett waved and replied in Spanish, "May all your dreams be pleasant."

After the upper-class students had filed out, the younger children got up quietly from their desks and followed the older ones outside. None of them spoke until Carol called from the door, "We're counting on you!"

"Yeah, that's right." Michael smiled. "We kinda like being all together."

Just then Ginger passed through the room. She said nothing, only waved. At the door, she raced out to the playground.

For the next ten minutes, Ophelia Bennett could hear the distant voices of the children on the playground, but inside, quietness prevailed. She opened her daily plan book and began to write mechanically, aware that her mind still focused on the immediate problem of the upper grades. *Oh, dear Heavenly Father,* she prayed silently, *I know You are going to give me wisdom. Give me such loving wisdom that I may also help Edwina.*

She had been thinking and praying all afternoon and no solution had seemed quite right. As she continued to petition God, a quiet assurance filled her heart. God had heard her; inspiration would come.

*

Mrs. Bennett hadn't been aware of Edwina Perkins coming into the room until the teacher plopped down on the chair next to her desk. Her pompadour had fallen from its place. Hairs hung limply down her perspiring forehead.

"Excuse me—"

"My dear, you look absolutely worn out."

"I am! And, look, I'm sorry I walked out in a huff this morning. I suppose I came back to school too soon. My doctor suggested that I wait another week. I also have high blood pressure and he knows the stress I've had here at North Prairie. I came back—I mean, I felt you needed me—and look." Her eyes glistened with tears. "Your classroom remained quiet all day. School is over and you're still calm and you look as fresh as you did when you arrived this morning."

"You are an extremely conscientious person. I value that quality."

"Not only are you calm and fresh, but you had two weeks with these monsters. I don't understand it, but they learned—or something since last summer. Even with all the trouble they gave me, they read and spelled and did arithmetic like I never saw before. Why, even that stu—that Max—actually understood what he was reading."

Ophelia studied the other teacher, then abruptly cocked her head slightly and focused her eyes on the ceiling.

"I don't believe you've listened to anything I've said—"

"Oh, I have been listening and I have heard every word. But my mind has raced ahead. I have decided on a plan. And yes, I am convinced that it will succeed and everyone will benefit."

"A plan? Look, I'm too tired for any new plan today. Those kids wore me out. I just want to get home, soak in a hot tub, listen to the radio, forget I'm a teacher, and maybe by tomorrow morning, I can—"

"Please, wait until you hear what I have in mind! Yes! Yes, I know it will succeed. And you will enjoy teaching as you never have before." Mrs. Bennett's hands moved as the tempo of her words increased. "I have this wonderful idea. It will work, because I know you love teaching school, even though you had a terrible time today."

"Yes, yes, that's true. A terrible, horrible, impossible day." The tears finally streamed down Miss Perkins's cheeks. "I'm such a failure, but teaching is the only thing I have ever wanted to do. Ever since I was a child, I—"

"From childhood I also felt that way as well. Some of us are born to teach. Now, listen, because I want to help you enjoy it here. I sense that you are an excellent teacher."

"I really showed *that* today, didn't I? I couldn't even control—"

"So I am prepared to make an arrangement with you."

"An arrangement?" Miss Perkins peered at the other teacher. She took out a white handkerchief, which she kept tucked under her left sleeve, and wiped her face.

"If you do not like the word *arrangement,* we can call it something else. Oh, Edwina, I have decided to let you join with me in making this school fun."

"Fun! Fun! I think we've had enough of *that* for one day. I mean—"

"Do not be shocked, my dear. Just look around my classroom. Tell me what you see that is different from the two previous years. Look! What is going on in here?"

Miss Perkins frowned. "I don't know. It was so quiet in here and the pictures on the walls that the kids drew and—"

"That is only evidence of what has been going on."

"Respect," she blurted out. "They respect you. I've never seen that before at North Prairie and—"

"Let me answer then. You yourself said the children learned. Even during the two weeks you were not here, all of the upper-class students learned. You noticed that Max can read, and that is true. Did you also observe how much

Nickolas has absorbed? And especially, I hope you observed that Yvonne has—"

"Well, yes. That's what I meant, I suppose." Miss Perkins eased out of her chair and moved around the room. She squinted at partially finished objects of papier-mâché. On another table someone had begun making a human skeleton out of clay, and although miniature in size, she commented on the accuracy. She turned and stared at the blackboard. Every child had a construction-paper face with a tongue sticking out taped on the board. Several black dots marred most of the tongues.

"What's that?"

"Read the sign below the faces."

In large, black letters, Ophelia had printed these words:

For murdering the English, I'm not hung;
But a black mark is placed upon my tongue.

"A black mark?"

"Yes, and it works. It truly works!" Mrs. Bennett walked across the room. "It is my informal method—a fun way—to teach them grammar. You see, they learn so much more if they teach themselves and they learn by listening to each other."

"Hmph. I never thought of grammar as fun. It's the hardest subject I teach each year!"

Ophelia went on. "This game, this method, is quite simple. That is part of the reason it is such a vibrant tool. It is extremely easy and all of them understand. You see, whenever a child makes a grammatical error and another child catches it, the first one who hears the mistake goes up to the board and places a black mark on the offender's tongue."

"And that works? Surely you—" Miss Perkins's mouth opened wide. "Yes, it does. I noticed today in class, even with all the chaos, that when they made grammatical mistakes they corrected themselves immediately."

"Yes, that's the new rule I started Friday. If a child catches himself immediately, before he finishes the sentence, no one is allowed to give him a black mark."

"Amazing. And it is effective, isn't it?"

"Yes, and they start with a grade of 100 and each black mark lowers them one point. Each week they start with a grade of 100 again. I can assure you—I have used this before—that by spring, we shall not have to use the black marks. Everyone, even the first graders, will end with at least 95 every week."

"And it works? It really does?"

"Yes, and quite well. They do most of the teaching to each other. I have variations of this game if they grow tired of it before they have all reached those high marks. I shall also tell you this much. By Christmas vacation, we shall not need to teach grammar to any of the students—and that includes even first graders."

"But I don't see how..."

"They learn by absorbing. By playing. By listening to each other. After all, isn't English first of all a spoken language and not merely for reading? And, of course, English is not the only subject for which I have developed games."

"Hmm, you know, I think I can understand how—" Miss Perkins stared at the comic faces. "Yes, I do understand."

"We can have such a lovely arrangement with all the students. If you agree to my methods, I assure you—I promise you—that you will have as much fun as the children. School will no longer be a horrid place to come to every day. You will love teaching and your latent talents will emerge." She stopped talking and stared into the younger woman's face. "You are extremely gifted as a teacher. You are, even though you do not believe it. That is, you do not believe it *yet.* But you will believe it, just as the children have begun to believe in themselves."

Edwina plopped into a student's seat. She shook her head and murmured, "I don't know that I could ever, ever think of school as fun."

"But it can be. And it will be. Please trust my initiative and allow me to have the opportunity to show you. The children were more skeptical than you are, but they were convinced before the end of the second day."

"The second day? By then, I've barely gotten them disciplined enough to—"

"Here is something to prove it to you. The annual achievement tests we give? You usually give it in the spring at North Prairie, do you not?"

"Yes, of course. So do most of the schools. They're always below grade."

"This year they will be ready by Christmas. And every child will be above grade level."

"Impossible!"

"Not the way these children have absorbed information. Please allow me the opportunity to demonstrate this tomorrow."

"Well—"

"Splendid," Ophelia said, accepting that single word as consent. "Now, I do have some simple advice for you. You must go home and relax. Take that bath. Listen to the radio. Tonight, Lionel Barrymore is going to narrate

Treasure Island. Whatever you do, you must not worry about tomorrow's lesson plans. By the time you arrive, I shall have them prepared for you."

"I know you're more experienced and all, but—"

"Yes, I am." She took the younger woman's hands in hers. "You see, my dear, God has been gracious to me and given me an unusual ability." She laughed self-consciously. "I suppose I sound quite boastful, but that is not the case, I assure you. What I am able to do, I do because of the gifts God has given me."

Miss Perkins's small eyes bulged in amazement. "I've never heard anyone talk like that before."

"Perhaps not. But no matter. When you arrive tomorrow—and if you could get here perhaps ten minutes early, that would be wonderful—I shall have everything worked out. You will catch on so quickly that before long you will develop ideas of your own on how to teach informally."

"That'll be the day!"

"Yes, that will be indeed. It will be a wonderful day, Edwina dear." Mrs. Bennett hugged the shorter teacher. "You will do splendidly; I know you will. I have the ability to see such talents in other people. You have such good qualities in you...qualities begging to be released and used to help others."

Edwina flushed. "I'm really not much of a teacher."

"You will become one, and you must leave everything to me. My dear, you will enjoy this."

"All right. I'll give it a try. What should I do tomorrow?"

"You start with the upper grades in your room and check attendance. Then you bring them into this room. Give me complete freedom. And, by the end of one full week, if you are not happier and more excited about teaching, and if the children are not learning beyond your expectations, I shall do anything you want. I shall give you complete freedom to tell *me* what to do. I am convinced that I have something—"

"This sounds incredulous to me...oh, I mean, not that you—"

"I understand your hesitancy. You see, I had an unhappy experience in school as a child. I wanted very much to learn, but I hated the dull sessions and even duller teachers. I made a promise to myself that one day I would become a teacher. And I asked God to help me so that I never, ever bored the children or caused them to lose their spontaneity. And in that atmosphere, I knew they would learn."

Ophelia handed Edwina essays written by Boy, Ginger, and Marvin. "Look at them. Can you believe how far these children have come already?"

Edwina's eyes skimmed Marvin's essay. "He was always the best—"

"Read the other two."

Edwina read them and her eyes lit up. "I can hardly believe—"

"Now you see the proof. For two weeks I have worked with these thirty-three children. We have had a grand time and they have also learned. Especially, you must watch Yvonne. That child is a gifted teacher. Mark my words on that. Best of all, we have had no discipline problems since the first day of school."

"None? How is that possible?"

"You will see."

"But how did you figure all this out? I mean, where did you get your ideas? I mean, aside from God, uh, helping you."

"I devised my own system of teaching and it succeeds beautifully. Actually, it is not all mine. I picked up ideas from the great professor John Dewey because I studied under him in Chicago, and then I picked up ideas from a Swiss educator named Jean Piaget. The point is, my methods prove their effectiveness. It is fun for the children and for the teacher. And when achievement tests come around, you will see the results."

"But with thirty-three monsters like these? If we had a lot of well-behaved students, I could—"

"That is exactly my point, my dear," replied Ophelia as she paced the room. "These youngsters are still fresh. Teachers regiment children into sitting straight and try to make them think like everyone else. Each child becomes like a puppet. I allow freedom—the freedom of movement—but mostly the freedom to learn. We have noise in the room most of the time, but it doesn't interfere with learning. And I help each child learn at his or her own pace. Even I learn. Professor Dewey called it discovery learning."

"Okay." Edwina shrugged. "I've agreed, but I have my reservations. I want you to know that before we start."

"All right. Let me show you." Ophelia moved to her desk, shuffled through a stack of papers and handed one of them to Miss Perkins. "Read it."

Our School

> Our school is fun this year. We do not learn by memorizing or saying stupid things all the time. We make up games and I already understand algebra. I like going to school now but I hated it before and my mother made me go every day. Now I can read and write and by the end of the year I want to read *Moby Dick* by myself.
>
> Max

"His spelling! And his penmanship." Miss Perkins studied the paper and read it again. "Are you sure Marvin didn't write this? Marvin's the best pupil in the class. But Max—"

"No, my dear, Marvin's essay is really better, much, much better. That is because Marvin has had more background. I can show you another paper he wrote. You see, he volunteered to conduct an experiment with bees. He has shown rare insight into scientific research. He has a fine, analytical mind."

The tiny, brown eyes opened wide. "I don't understand, but all right. Just one thing I want to be clear about. What if this program of yours doesn't work?"

"It will. We had two weeks during your sickness. And Edwina, you will learn. You are a fine, able teacher. I know that without seeing you in action. It is something I know inside. By the end of this year, you will be accepted *and recognized* as an excellent teacher."

Miss Perkins closed her eyes. "Oh, if only..."

9

THANKSGIVING HOLIDAYS ALWAYS MARKED A SIGNIFICANT TIME at North Prairie School with no classes from Wednesday evening until the following Monday. Many families made plans to visit relatives or take short trips. Next to the days before Christmas vacation, it had always been the worst time of year for Miss Perkins. She often said that she ought to let them leave a week early for all the teaching she was able to do from Monday until Wednesday.

This year, it was different. That was when she knew beyond any doubt that the experiment she had been bullied into—and she had resented Ophelia for always being right—was a success.

"But, Miss Perkins, why can't we come to school? I mean, just for a little while?" Nickolas asked. "I'm not going away during the vacation period."

She smiled and tousled Nickolas's hair before answering. " 'Fraid not. Part of growing up means learning to accept life the way it is. The days away from school will be good for you. When you return next week, you'll be even more eager to learn."

"I couldn't be any more eager than I am now," Max called out from the back of the room. Heads turned quickly. This was the first time Max had spoken up without being prodded.

Mrs. Bennett, busy playing a phonics game with the first and second graders, looked up, smiled, and turned her attention once more to the younger children.

"Aw, nuts," Nickolas said. "This isn't fair. When I didn't want to learn, I had to come. Now that I want to come, you won't let me." Then he grinned.

The others laughed, but Karen laughed louder and longer while she gazed into his eyes.

"Don't forget, today before you leave, you have an assignment to finish—the annual essay writing contest for the unincorporated schools of Lake County." Miss Perkins paused long enough to glance at Marvin. He received one of her warmest smiles. "We're always proud of Marvin because he has won first place for the past two years. I'd like to see the rest of you enter and possibly make an honorable mention."

"Or even win!" Max yelled.

"Uh, yes, of course. Even win," she said and tried to muster enthusiasm.

"It is open to every child from fourth grade up."

"Maybe I might even win first place!" Max persisted.

"Why, yes...yes, of course," cooed Miss Perkins. "Nothing's automatic about Marvin's winning. The rest of you have an excellent chance of competing with him."

"I didn't mean competing," Max said. "I wouldn't write for that reason—not to win *over* somebody else—just to win."

"Yes, uh, yes, of course. We all must have our goals to aim for."

Max's face hardened. "And you think that—"

"Miss Perkins and Mrs. Bennett," Ginger interrupted and raised her hand. "My mother wants to know why I don't bring school books home—you know, like English and spelling, instead of just reading books. She keeps saying we always did before. Besides, she also keeps saying she doesn't think we're getting much out of school this year unless I bring papers home and show what we did."

"I hear the same thing almost every day," Stephen said.

"When I tried to explain to her about learning Spanish, my mother said that could wait until high school or even college," Ginger said.

"Yeah, my old man—uh, my dad—he says the same thing," Boy added.

"Boy made a mistake!" squealed Michael Hege. "Boy made a mistake! He said 'my dad he' and that's wrong." He raced to the board and drew a heavy black mark on Boy's tongue.

"You're right!" Boy saluted his young friend.

"Ginger, in answer to your question," Mrs. Bennett said, pausing in her instructions to the first and second graders, "You do not need to take home papers. I realize you did in previous years. I also know that many of your parents struggled through your arithmetic and spelling with you. You spent a lot of time on homework but I do not believe that you children learned much. I suspect your parents received a lot of reviewing."

Marvin laughed. "Hey, how did you know?"

"You are all doing so well—every one of you—so none of you needs to take work home."

"Yeah, but my mother insists," Ginger said, jutting out her bottom lip. "Please help me know what to do or how to handle her."

"Hmmm, in that case, take one or two reading books home with you. You are a bright girl, Ginger. It's time you began reading the classics. I think *Little Women* might be appropriate. Or *Pride and Prejudice*. Perhaps you and Karen might want to dramatize one of the scenes from *Little Women* to perform one noon period when the weather is too inclement to go outside."

"Okay, Mrs. Bennett, I'll read *Little Women*—because you say so. But my mother really wants me to bring home my spelling or something like that."

"My folks don't think I'm learning either," Larry said. "My dad keeps saying that anytime I want to go to school, something's wrong and that we must be making everything miserable for you and that we're certainly not learning nothing."

"Double negative, Miss Perkins." Karen stood. "Larry used a double negative—'not learning nothing.' He should have said, 'Not learning anything.' "

"Right! Larry, a black mark on your tongue," Miss Perkins said from across the room. "Karen, you get a point on the grade board."

"Thank you—"

"Hmmm, Karen, this week you've already caught eight mistakes. Sharp ears," Miss Perkins added.

"And it *is* fun too."

"Anyway," Larry said with a slight edge to his voice after Karen marked a dot on his paper tongue, "my parents don't seem to understand what's going on. I don't mind taking books home."

"I suppose we shall have to make changes," Mrs. Bennett said wistfully. "I knew it would come. It always does."

"What do you mean, 'It always does?' " the freckle-faced first grader asked.

"Only that parents never seem to understand new concepts in education. Too many think learning comes only by sheer drudgery." Mrs. Bennett shrugged her thin shoulders and almost immediately her face brightened again. "All right, you may each take a book home. But—"

Everyone looked at her.

"*But*—and listen carefully—it must be in the subject where you're the weakest. Before you leave for vacation, let me know which book you will take home and then we shall write down what you plan to do for homework. I shall expect to see the completed work either on my desk or Miss Perkins's on Monday."

"My mother does not ask for homework," Yvonne said, "but I would be pleased to take an English book home with me."

Mrs. Bennett smiled at the Mexican girl. "Very wise. You have made fine progress so far. You used to get more black marks than anyone else in the classroom. But, look, only one mark this week."

"And after this short vacation, not one mark—not ever again!"

"Yes, Yvonne, you will soon speak the English language that well. You try so hard, and we are all able to rejoice with you in observing the results. Hard work always pays off." Mrs. Bennett's eyes misted.

"Did I say something wrong?" Yvonne asked.

"Wrong? No, no, of course not. I was only thinking of you students. In my eighteen years of teaching, I have never seen such amazing progress in such a brief period of time." She stood and gazed around the room. "I knew you were a special class, but I did not realize how special until just now. I knew you would do well, but you have exceeded my expectations. I am extremely proud of you."

"We like you, Mrs. Bennett. Better'n any teacher we ever had before," Marvin called out.

"And...uh, of course, we like Miss Perkins, too." Max smiled at the shorter teacher.

Miss Perkins flushed and examined her fingernails. No student had ever said those words before.

10

THREE INCHES OF SNOW FELL THANKSGIVING MORNING and began to melt on Friday. By Saturday all traces had disappeared. Monday brought an overcast sky and unleashed the northern winds. Whenever the classroom became momentarily quiet, the outside roaring reminded the students of the sinking temperatures. They went out to play at recess, but the cold air and continuous blasts of icy chill soon forced them back inside.

After eating lunch, Miss Perkins instructed each child. "You each bundle up, run outside and around the building twice if you're in grades one through four. The rest of you will run three times."

Minutes later, the children all returned, laughing and teasing.

"And I ran three times just like the big kids," Michael said.

"We all did," Stephen said. "And I was almost as fast as Susan."

"You were not," she said. "Well, all right, about as fast."

"And now we enter once again in our warm refuge," Karen said.

"What movie did you pick that line from?" Nickolas asked.

*

At afternoon recess, the children returned from their outside run, hung up their coats and scarves, removed their boots, and returned to their lessons. No one heard the Buick Dynaflow pull up, but they all felt the chill that swept through the building as the door opened. Most of them, absorbed in their studies, didn't look up when they heard the door slam shut. They did look up as they heard two pairs of feet walking heavily across the room.

Karen greeted them loudly. "Hello, Mr. Pettygill."

"Yes, hello, good to see you again," he replied and nodded, obviously not knowing who she was. Although stocky, his height tended to hide that fact. His hair, clipped short at the sides and top, had a silvery sheen.

As he moved toward Mrs. Bennett's desk, he removed his hat, scarf, and overcoat. The other younger man, who was hatless, unbuttoned his overcoat and followed.

"Hmm, very wise," Mr. Pettygill mumbled, "very wise, Mrs. Bennett. Moving everyone into one room in this cold weather. Makes the fuel go further. Very economical. I'm pleased at such measures."

"Mr. Pettygill, it is good of you to visit our classroom." Mrs. Bennett rose from a kneeling position on the floor where she had been playing a subtraction game with the second graders.

"For weeks I have intended to visit your school," he said with his deep but pleasant voice. "I have been, unfortunately, quite busy, you know. The work of superintendent makes constant demands." He stopped and his gaze swept over the classroom.

The children had halted their activities and stared at him.

"Boys and girls! Back to your books. I won't stay long, because I don't like to interrupt your studies. Time is valuable." He paced the room as though ready to begin a lecture. "Gain more knowledge. Make better people of yourselves."

Catherine giggled and hid her face. Max continued to stare. Mrs. Bennett glared at him until she caught his attention. She held up her index finger. The word *concentration* formed on her lips. He buried his head immediately.

Mr. Pettygill moved only his head and continued to observe the children. He smiled at Mrs. Bennett as if to say, "Well done," before he briefly acknowledged Miss Perkins. Then, almost as if the man hadn't existed before, the superintendent said, "And this—this is my assistant. Reginald Forder. One day I'll retire, you know." His attempt at a laugh succeeded only in a kind of grunt. "Uh, Mr. Forder used to be principal at Zion Elementary."

"I am quite happy to have you visit us with Mr. Pettygill." Mrs. Bennett extended her hand to the young man, half a foot shorter than she was. "You have a kind face."

He smiled, blushed, and his brown eyes sparkled. "Thank—thank you." He took her hand and shook it vigorously.

"I hope you will enjoy working with Mr. Pettygill," Mrs. Bennett said. "I've known him for nearly twenty years. He has improved the educational level of our county—"

"No need to say those kind words," Mr. Pettygill said, even though the beam on his face declared otherwise.

"Mr. Pettygill works quite hard and is an extremely diligent man. You can learn a great deal from him."

"Why, thank you, Mrs. Bennett." Sylvester Pettygill cleared his throat. "Very kind, very kind indeed." He cleared his throat once again. "Now, Mrs. Bennett, if I may have a few moments of your time," he said, ignoring Reginald.

They walked into Miss Perkins's classroom.

*

Reginald walked over to Miss Perkins. "Hello, I'm—"

"Yes, I—I know." She fidgeted with her belt. "I'm Edwina Perkins." She smiled as she looked into his eyes, only three inches above her own.

He hardly noticed her words, only the lovely even teeth and the small dark eyes. "Oh, I, uh, understand you've been teaching here—uh, three years."

Miss Perkins blushed and lowered her gaze. "Uh huh," she mumbled, "this is my third year."

"Mr. Pettygill said you graduated from Cedar Falls College." He gazed into her eyes again.

"Yes, yes, I did." She shifted her gaze to the side. "I graduated in 1936."

"Really? That's just two years after I earned my degree. Funny, I don't remember you in any of my education courses."

"Oh, I remember you!" she said. A tinge of red began with her neckline and spread upward. She turned toward the window. "We had four classes together. Uh, I mean, you know, three or four."

"How could I not have noticed you?"

"Why would you pay any attention to me?" she asked, still looking down. "You were always such a good student. And in Teaching Methods class, you gave the best presentation I ever saw and heard from a student and you edited the yearbook and assisted in the newspaper and were vice president of—" She flushed again, then added, "anyway, I remember you."

"Yes, you do." He grinned. "And I ought to have my vision checked for not remembering you."

*

The two of them talked, as if unaware of the presence of the thirty-three children. Yes, she remembered Reginald. She'd had a crush on him in college but had never told anyone.

She liked the strong chin line that became evident when he grinned; she'd noticed that back in college. For a short man, he had large teeth, although they didn't look out of place. It was only that she always associated large teeth with taller men. Most of all, she liked his hair. Although slightly thinning already, it was a soft, wavy ash blond. She had often wondered what it would be like to run her fingers through his hair. Not that she ever would, but in college she had daydreamed of it—often.

"I can't believe we had classes together. And yet I didn't remember you," Reginald said.

"You were always busy dating my friends, Eva Everson or Kathy Willis. Guess—guess you never noticed plain girls like me," Miss Perkins said, suddenly realizing she was twisting her handkerchief in her fingers.

Momentarily her mind flashed back to those few times she'd talked to him at college. She'd always seemed to be twisting a handkerchief in her nervous hands then, too. Had he noticed? She stopped abruptly and placed the handkerchief in her blouse pocket.

He smiled at her.

That's the look I wanted him to give me back at Cedar Falls, she thought. He's smiling at me. *At me.*

*

Mr. Pettygill, who had finished his brief words with Mrs. Bennett, came back into the room and stood next to Mr. Forder, surveying the room. "In a few minutes," he said softly, "we'll leave."

Mr. Pettygill ignored the curious eyes of the children and walked around much like a general inspecting his troops. With both hands clasped behind his back, he scrutinized the children and the classroom. He commented on the artwork.

Miss Perkins watched and inhaled sharply when Mr. Pettygill approached the faces with black tongues. He stared for several seconds and raised an eyebrow.

Mrs. Bennett explained the game and he listened as if giving her his full attention. "Yes, yes, I see," he replied, obviously not impressed.

He picked up his coat, which he had laid carefully across an empty chair, and began to put on his scarf. Turning toward Miss Perkins, he cleared his throat loudly.

Miss Perkins nudged Mr. Forder. "I think he's ready to leave."

Reginald pulled to attention and nodded. "Uh, nice talking to you, uh, Edwina, uh, Miss Perkins. I have to move on, but...perhaps I could talk with you some more. About Cedar Falls. I mean." He leaned slightly forward, lowering his voice. "I'd like to see your 1936 annual. You know, see if I remember anyone else from your class."

"I'd enjoy showing it to you—very much. Maybe you could come by—by my apartment—that is, if you want." And even though she no longer held her handkerchief, and even though her hands were behind her, she continued to twist the imaginary cloth around her fingers.

"I'd like that very much, Miss Perkins," he said as he straightened.

"I'm in the telephone book," she said as she flushed again. "I'm free any night...uh, well, you know, uh, frequently, I mean."

"I'll call you tonight." He tipped his head and smiled. "I can't believe I don't remember you."

To avoid embarrassing herself again, Miss Perkins turned quickly to her seventh and eighth graders. "All right now, let's name all 48 state capitals. You have five seconds to write down each answer. Ready...first, what city is the capital of New Mexico?"

*

Reginald walked toward the other side of the room where he joined Mrs. Bennett and Mr. Pettygill. The superintendent never stood in one spot but moved continually. Even when talking, one of his feet moved back and forth or to the side. He stared at a pile of essays on her desk and skimmed through them. "Hmm, excellent penmanship, my dear Mrs. Bennett. Excellent."

"My, yes," Reginald said as he stood over the desk, peered closely, and read them. "Especially these from the upper grades. I'm impressed. Very fine work."

"The students appear to be doing well," Mr. Pettygill stated loud enough for everyone to hear. Then, lowering his voice and facing Mrs. Bennett he said, almost under his breath, "I think, however, you waste too much time and effort on frills instead of learning basic skills. If you know what I mean."

"Yes, I know what you mean," she answered noncommittally.

"Otherwise"—and Sylvester Pettygill buttoned his overcoat and picked up his hat. "Otherwise, I think everything—"

He moved quickly to the third desk where Larry sat. He grabbed the contents out of the boy's hands. He stared at what he held, as though unable to believe his eyes. "Mrs. Bennett? Cards? Playing cards?"

"Yes, playing cards, Mr. Pettygill, but if you'll turn them over, you will see what they really are. They are for learning fractions, not for gambling. Larry worked quite faithfully on these. He took an old deck of cards from home—"

"But *cards!* Playing cards. Why, why such things can lead to bad habits."

"Not these cards, Mr. Pettygill. He's playing a game that Marvin introduced two weeks ago. A game Marvin thought out all by himself. He used it to help teach the third and fourth graders simple fractions. It works like this. You have to get enough fractions to make one whole and you can mix them, such as ½ and two ¼ cards, or whatever combination you can figure out. He made additional cards and rules for upper grades—"

"Yes, yes."

"They have to reduce fractions and they gain additional points by multiplying and dividing them. The sixth through eighth graders must also be able to convert to percentages and decimals. Larry used that idea, made his own set, and glued them—"

"But he glued them on *playing cards!*"

"Very clever of the boy." Reginald took the cards from Mr. Pettygill's hand and glanced through them. "Certainly shows a clear mind. The figures are nicely printed, too."

"Yes, and the children have learned—" Mrs. Bennett interjected.

"Most of the students can now change from fractions to percentages in their heads," Miss Perkins called out from her end of the room. "Don't you think that's quite an accomplishment?"

"Yes...yes, I suppose so," Mr. Pettygill admitted, although his frown did not leave. "However, I hope that in the future, he'll either do games such as this at home or at least use something other than *playing cards*." Sylvester carefully smoothed the scarf around his neck and raised the collar of his overcoat slightly.

Reginald handed the cards back, patted Larry's shoulder, and smiled. "Keep that up, young man, and you'll be after my job, won't you?"

"Mister Forder! We must leave now." Mr. Pettygill peered at each desk as he moved closer to the door. "Good-bye, Mrs. Bennett." He opened the door without glancing back.

"And, good-bye, Miss Perkins," Reginald called. "I'll see you again."

*

Ginger snickered, punched Catherine, and both of them giggled. Karen turned to the others and went, "Shh, I think it's lovely. Just lovely the way they parted, like the way Joan Crawford said good-bye to Franchot Tone in *The Bride Wore Red.*"

"Oh, it's love-love-love-ly, all right." Nickolas guffawed.

Miss Perkins blushed as she twisted the retrieved handkerchief once again.

Larry turned to Mrs. Bennett as soon as the door slammed. "I'm sorry, honest. I didn't mean to cause trouble. I want to know fractions so I can play with the bigger kids."

"It is perfectly all right. You did nothing wrong—nothing wrong whatsoever." But she did not look at him, only down at her desk.

"I won't do it again. I mean, if visitors come like Mr. Pettygill, I won't have them out so they can catch me."

Mrs. Bennett left her desk, came over to Larry, and patted his hand. "You do not need to apologize. It is not your fault. If it had not been your cards, it would have been something else." She added to herself, "Always something."

"I don't know what you mean."

"Only that it's not your fault. It is all right, I assure you. If it had not been you, one of the other children would have said something amiss. Or it would have occurred on another day." She walked over to the window, leaned her head against the pane, and closed her eyes.

"Is Mrs. Bennett sick?" Ginger whispered.

"No, you ninny, I think she's praying," Nickolas replied.

"Mrs. Bennett! Mrs. Bennett! Don't feel bad, please," Larry said. "I like this school. I've had more fun in your school than I ever had in my whole life."

Miss Perkins looked up, abruptly breaking her thoughts away from Reginald's thinning ash-blond hair. She smiled.

"Yeah, because you're the best teacher. You're the only teacher I've ever liked."

Miss Perkins stopped smiling.

"Why can't we go home and tell our parents all the fun we're having and all the good things we're doing?" Larry asked.

"Because," Ophelia said as she turned and faced the class. She kept the back of her head pressed against the window and shivered, as though the blast of cold air was snaking its way down her back. "Because most adults are unable to believe learning can be fun or that it can be easy. But they will believe—one day your parents will believe."

"Oh, I certainly hope so," Karen said.

"One day, they will know. Perhaps God will let you be the ones to show them."

11

COLD WINDS, WHICH BEGAN IN LATE NOVEMBER, swept through the North Prairie area in December of 1940. Although little snow fell that month, the temperature plummeted to sub-zero levels. The school, located on a flat plain with no hills for more than three miles in any direction, received the full impact of the wintry forces. Biting winds nipped at the school building. The wind dropped during the morning and strong air currents swept through the upper atmosphere and pushed the massed clouds eastward.

Drafts swirled through the two-room school. Even the potbellied stoves could not keep the rooms warm enough. Most children wore two pairs of socks and a sweater or two shirts. But because of their absorption with their studies, they seldom complained about the cold.

The two teachers reacted differently. Other than wearing anklets over her silk stockings, Edwina Perkins scarcely seemed aware of the problem. Mrs. Bennett, however, keenly felt the cold and kept herself moving so she would not have to sit still and feel the cold air rushing across the classroom.

Two weeks before the Christmas vacation, Mrs. Bennett arrived early on Thursday morning. The janitor had started fires in both stoves and the heat was already beginning to chase away the chill of the night. She sat at her desk, looking at the still-empty desks.

"Maybe this time it will be different," she said aloud. "Maybe this time they will understand. Please, Lord, let it work out. I have tried so hard. And each time it has ended the same way. But this year I have such a special class. Please...please do not let it end the way the others have." Tears slid down her cheeks and she wiped them away.

She remained at her desk several minutes and said nothing, waiting as though God would speak to her. She heard no voice. Then she remembered that Jesus had prayed in the Garden of Gethsemane. He had asked the Father not to make Him go through His suffering and cried out in final surrender, "Not My will, but Thine."

"Yes, Lord," she whispered. "Whatever you want, I am willing."

Still seated, she allowed her mind to retrace the events of the previous evening. It had been the December PTA. Several of the parents, even of older children, called her aside and talked with her.

"I've never seen my son enjoy school so much. You teachers here must be doing a fine job this year."

"Karen thinks you're the best teacher in the world, even though, of course, she's in Miss Perkins's class."

Mrs. Bagnull had commented as she left, "Marvin informs me that he is doing well this year. I appreciate your support of Miss Perkins's work. It delights me to know that my son is already mastering geometry and he's barely in the eighth grade."

Yvonne's mother had come to the December meeting, smiled at Mrs. Bennett, and said several times in Spanish how thankful she was for the help her daughter had received.

Max's aunt came, too. She said almost nothing to anyone unless asked a question and then her answers were brief and often monosyllabic. She did say, "Thank you for helping him." She was the first one to leave.

But on that Thursday morning Mrs. Bennett didn't worry about Yvonne's mother or Max's aunt. They knew, somehow, that the children had received help—an extraordinary amount of assistance. They expressed it as well as they knew how. In their gratefulness, they never stopped to question her methods or even cared. They had seen results. But it was the parents of the better students that troubled her. They were ambitious. Difficult.

And they will become my enemies.

"Do not let my heart fail me, dear Father," she whispered in the silence of her empty classroom. "Fill my heart with love for them so that I may please You when the tests come. I ask, but I know, North Prairie will not be different from the other schools. I imagine North Prairie will be the same as Winthrop Harbor, Culver, North Chicago, or Benton. Trouble might not come right away. Maybe I shall even stay three or four years. But it always comes."

Ophelia sighed. It never occurred to her to ask herself or God if it was worth it. She knew what she had to do. She and Richard had made that contract in the beginning of their marriage. Even though he could not live up to it now, she could—and would.

She patted her hair, coaxing a stray wisp back into the bun. But this morning, even before the children arrived, tiredness crept over her. The weariness came from more than the cold weather. More than the responsibility of keeping up with thirty-three pupils and another teacher.

"Well, Ophelia, you have turned forty-six," she said aloud. "You cannot expect to keep acting the way you did at twenty-six. Slow down." But even as she said the words to herself, and despite knowing the words were true, she had no intention of slowing down. She would push herself even harder this year, even though she knew there was gray in her once dark red hair.

"I am going according to my plan. As long as I can teach unhindered, I shall expend my energies without reservation. I can relax later." She banged her fist on the desk and said aloud once again, "And right now I can also stop feeling sorry for myself."

*

Four days before Christmas vacation, Ophelia Bennett sat at her desk while the children continued to work on projects and lessons begun the day before.

She waited for the arrival of Reginald Forder, for a different reason than Edwina Perkins. Mr. Forder had been assigned to administer achievement tests at North Prairie School this year, which would use up most of the morning. He would take the tests back to his own office and score them during the Christmas vacation period. Previously, teachers had administered and scored their own achievement tests, but hints of cheating had changed the procedure. One teacher in Waukegan had been caught teaching her class directly from the test itself. "This will not happen this year," Mr. Pettygill had announced, "or ever again in Lake County."

While she awaited Reginald's arrival, she knew he would bring something else: a list of county winners in the annual essay contest. All students above third grade had to enter, but each year, predictably, the seventh and eighth graders received the awards.

Marvin had won while he was still a sixth grader (the first time anyone could recall that happening), and again last year during the seventh grade. She already had been invited to a party Mrs. Bagnull had arranged "in case Marvin wins." She stared at the invitation that lay on her desk and smiled to herself at the ploy Mrs. Bagnull had used. It was an invitation to a Christmas party honoring those who participated in the annual essay-writing contest.

The children, alerted that Mr. Forder would be visiting that morning, quietly walked to their places when they heard his car pulling up. Several snickered at Miss Perkins, who just "happened" to be near the door when Mr. Forder came into the school.

*

"Hello, Miss Perkins. How nice to see you again," he said and smiled. "Perhaps you can help me by passing out the tests while I get myself ready."

"Of course, Mr. Forder," she replied too loudly. Her hand touched Mr.

Forder's. She winced slightly at his cold fingers but smiled when he did not move his hand away immediately. They stared momentarily into each others' eyes.

A student behind her coughed and another giggled. Miss Perkins jerked her hand away, flushed, and in so doing, dropped most of the papers. "Oh, I'm sorry," she said as she bent and began picking them up.

Reginald bent beside her and helped her retrieve the tests. As he moved close to her, still half-bent, he whispered, "You're beautiful, Edwina."

She could feel her face turn crimson and rose swiftly to her feet. "It's a bit hot in here, I think." She hurried to her own desk to sort out tests by grades.

Once sorted, Edwina passed out the tests and checked to make certain that every pupil had two sharp pencils and an eraser. Mr. Forder took off his coat and scarf, hung them over an empty chair, and went directly to Mrs. Bennett's desk. He handed her an envelope. He winked before he faced the class.

Edwina watched Mrs. Bennett's fingers shake as she tore the envelope open, unfolded the paper, and scanned the list. A faint smile appeared on her face. She laid the paper aside.

"Aren't you going to tell us? You know, about who won," Karen asked. "Did Marvin win again?"

"Please, Mrs. Bennett, won't you tell us?" the freckle-faced boy pleaded.

"Not at the moment. You have all waited a full month for this list. It will be here on my desk after your examinations."

"Yes, children," Miss Perkins said. "That will come later. Now you must focus and I know you will all do well."

"Worth a try," Susan said, just loud enough for everyone to hear.

Miss Perkins put her right index finger to her lips.

The preliminary instructions began and the children listened carefully to Mr. Forder's words. Edwina Perkins scarcely heard what he said; she was enamored by his voice—exactly as it had sounded at Cedar Falls.

Strange, he had paid no attention to her then. Yet since that day he came in with Mr. Pettygill, he had called her on the telephone five times and had visited her apartment three times, always keeping the door open so that anyone could see there was no impropriety. Before he left after his third visit, he had taken her hand and they had stared for a long time into each other's eyes. Then he kissed her—softly, gently—and she wanted to hold him and not let go. She couldn't, of course, but she longed for his next visit.

As her adoring eyes fixed on Mr. Pettygill's assistant, she realized she loved him. Had it been love at Cedar Falls? Or hero worship? Or had it happened when he called her on the telephone the first time and spoke for nearly an hour?

Then she wondered why Reginald had suddenly noticed her. What was different about her now? She was still overweight, although she had successfully lost eight pounds since Reginald came into her life. Her corset certainly fit better and Mrs. Bennett had said, "You look so much more slender, my dear."

It doesn't matter, she thought. She turned toward him. Whenever he glanced her way, she smiled.

*

Ophelia Bennett rose from her desk, walked to the rear of the classroom, tapped Edwina Perkins on the shoulder, and the two walked into the other classroom. The stove had been lit and coal piled in, but the room had not warmed yet. They pulled up two chairs near the fire.

"You are truly different from the first day you came back to school. Perhaps you have not noticed it, but you are like another person—like a prisoner set free."

"But—" Edwina asked quizzically.

"Are you wondering why he never noticed you at college? Because you were just another student then—shy, self-conscious, and hardly the type who attracted him. Now you are different. You have developed into a good teacher. Daily you grow more confident in your work. You walk differently and when you smile, you have a most attractive smile. The children respect you as a teacher."

"Oh, no they don't. Not the way they respect you. Oh, I didn't mean it that way, only—"

"But you are quite correct, my dear." She smiled at Edwina Perkins. "One day you'll be known as *the* teacher at North Prairie. People will admire your work and appreciate your ideas—and you have them. You truly do and you have begun to demonstrate a delightful creative imagination."

"You did it. I couldn't have done anything without your help."

"You only needed someone to help bring your ideas into the open—to make you aware of your ability. I am thankful to God to have been chosen for that task."

"You've done so much for me—"

"Now, I am going to prepare exercises for this afternoon." She raised the palm of her right hand to cut off the conversation. "This is a new reading game for those first graders to help them with their diphthongs. Right now, don't you think you could be of assistance if you went into the other classroom and assisted Mr. Forder? He might need your help."

"Yes, in case he needs me." Impulsively she hugged Mrs. Bennett and then pulled back in shock. "I'm so sorry. I didn't mean to—"

"Why would you choose to apologize? I am pleased that you embraced me. I am just as pleased that you were free enough to do so. You see," she stopped and her eyes twinkled, "you *are* the prisoner set free!"

12

"AND NOW, CLASS, YOUR ATTENTION. Miss Perkins will assist Mr. Forder in collecting the achievement tests and take them to his car." Mrs. Bennett waited until the tests had been collected and the two had gone outside. "Now for the big event of the day. I know each of you is interested in the results of the Lake County Essay Contest."

The children all tried to huddle around Mrs. Bennett's desk as she held the folded paper in front of her. "First, Mr. Pettygill says these are the best essays submitted in any year in Lake County."

"But did any of us win?" Max asked.

"There are three winners, as usual, and a list of honorable mentions. I am proud to announce that of the ten honorable mentions, the names of five students in this school appear."

"Which ones?" Ginger asked, stars dancing in her eyes.

"The list of winners begins. First place: Max Richard Waxman."

"Ohh, Max, you did it!" Ginger gushed. "You are wonderful." She clasped his hand and then, embarrassed, pulled back.

Cheers and happy noises ascended and then quickly subsided as Mrs. Bennett raised her palm. "Second prize to Charles Richard Hartman of Winthrop Harbor. Third prize to Ralph Edward Blakely, Wadsworth School. First honorable mention to Marvin Eugene Bagnull Jr.—"

"Only first honorable *mention?*" Marvin asked, tears already filling his eyes. "My mother will skin me."

"You have won first place two years in a row. That is quite an achievement, and now you are first honorable mention. I would say that is a splendid three-year record."

"Yeah, but it isn't first place."

"No, Marvin, it is not first place. Now then," and Ophelia Bennett continued reading the list, "for sixth honorable mention, Nickolas Marshall Harrison."

"Are you sure? I never won anything before in my life!"

"You have won now, Nickolas. And we're proud of you."

Karen and Boy placed eighth and ninth honorable mentions.

"And here is the name of one that I believe has made extraordinary progress this year. Yvonne Ortega has received tenth honorable mention."

Yvonne screamed. "Me? It is not—not possible!"

"She should have said 'I,' " Ginger called out, "and not 'me.' "

"I mean, how is that possible? How could I have such earned an honor?"

"Because you worked hard, really hard," Max said. "Both of us did!"

Ophelia Bennett waited while they squealed and congratulated one another. She watched the pain in Marvin's face. In the years ahead, this would be an invaluable lesson for him, but it would take a long time for him to appreciate the results of this contest. For now, he hurt deeply—mainly because he had disappointed his parents. She wished she could ease the hurt, but it was something he had to battle himself.

"Children, I am proud of you all. Every single one of you. Even those of you who did not win tried very hard. I read your essays but the rules said I could not speak to you about them. Your work showed much thought and effort. I would have wished to give each of you a prize."

*

Outside, the wind sweeping across the open field propelled the two figures toward the parked 1938 Chevrolet. Edwina Perkins quickly hopped inside and Reginald ran around to the other side and let himself in. As soon as he sat down, he pulled a woolen blanket out of the back seat and spread it across Edwina's legs. She smiled in appreciation.

"I think you're wonderful, Edwina, and every time I see you, you look even more wonderful." He leaned over and gently kissed her cold lips. "And you're one of the best teachers I've seen in Lake County. Probably the best, but maybe I'm prejudiced."

"I try. Honestly I try to—"

"Someday observers will come from all over the county—even all over the state—to see the things you're doing. Maybe Mr. Pettygill doesn't recognize your achievements, but I know you're changing things and those kids are producing. Why, right now, today, we could put those students of yours against any in Lake County—even in the state."

"It's not really my doings, Reginald. It's Mrs. Bennett. She's so clever and—"

Reginald quickly kissed her again. "That's another reason I love you, dear Edwina. You never boast about your achievements. I'm sure Mrs. Bennett must help, but you probably give her more than she gives you. After all, it's your students who are excelling. Here. Look at this list. It's a copy of the winners of the essay contest."

Edwina's eyes beamed as she read the listing. "My students?"

"Yes, yours, and see what a grand job you've done. Why, if you play things right, in a couple of years, who knows? Changes are beginning to take place in the field of education. The work of dedicated teachers like you is beginning to make a difference. You are boldly—courageously—standing up and showing the rest of us what can be done."

"Thank you," she murmured and squeezed his hand.

"But where did you learn all this? I saw evidence of all kinds of things the students did themselves. Games, artwork, the playing card games…"

"Oh, it's not really my work, Reginald. Just ideas I've—I've picked up."

"Not at Cedar Falls."

"No...from, uh, observing, listening, and thinking. I've done more reading since then. You know, people like Pestalozzi...Piaget...Dewey."

"None of whom received high marks at Cedar Falls."

"I guess you just have to keep growing or—you go backward," she said, pushing aside the guilt that nipped at her heart.

"You're marvelous, Edwina! Just marvelous!" Reginald kissed her a third time and held her much longer before he finally released her.

Later, when she returned to the classroom, Edwina Perkins hoped that the flush she felt on her face would not be noticed. Or, if the children noticed, that they'd assume the wind had caused it. She wanted to stand inside the door and relive the previous ten minutes in her memory. But she knew she had no time for that now.

"Miss Perkins! Miss Perkins!" Karen's yell broke through her thoughts. "Max won first prize! And I won eighth honorable mention!"

"Yes, I know. And I'm happy—absolutely happy!" She smiled at all the children. "You've done so well. I'm very, very proud of you all. But now, I want all of you to go outside for a few minutes and run around in the cold air. You've been sitting there writing all morning. You need a change."

*

The children ran to the cloakroom and grabbed for hats, boots, coats, and scarves. Even with all the laughing and playful pushing, the older ones helped the younger.

Yvonne didn't go to the cloakroom but walked up to Mrs. Bennett's desk. The teacher, absorbed in her own work, didn't look up. Yvonne opened her mouth to speak, then stood quietly and fidgeted with her hands.

Impulsively Yvonne's thin arms encircled the teacher. She kissed Mrs. Bennett on the cheek. "I love you, Teacher."

Then she raced toward the cloakroom.

Ophelia remained in the same position, but she lowered her eyes and said silently, *Moments like these, Lord, make all the heartaches worthwhile.*

And for a moment, the ominous events of the future seemed of no consequence to Ophelia Bennett. *This is right. I know it is.*

13

"I AM MARVIN BAGNULL'S MOTHER. We met at the PTA meeting," the voice said icily as she swept across the room and into the straight chair. She unbuttoned her heavy fur coat. "I presume you received my note this morning?"

"Yes, I did."

"Frankly, I'm upset, as you can well imagine. Marvin should have won first place and you know that as a fact. I've already contacted Mr. Pettygill about this whole affair. He says that since you are the principal he will let you judge the matter. If you agree, we can simply say it's a mistake and reverse the awards. It will only affect this school, not the whole county, but I can accept that."

"That would not be honest, would it?"

"Honest?" the dark-haired woman repeated, arching her right eyebrow, which had been plucked to a thin arc. "I don't see that honesty has anything to do with it. It's a matter of doing what's right, that's all!"

"And doing what is right means cheating Max Waxman out of his first achievement in life?"

"I'm sorry I was rude and I'm certain it sounds terrible the way I've been talking. Let me start again." Mrs. Bagnull leaned back in her chair and made an attempt to relax as she slowly peeled off her long, skin-tight leather gloves. The muscles around her thin mouth remained tight even when she attempted to smile. "Marvin's a brilliant young man."

"Extremely. He has one of the finest minds I have ever seen in my eighteen years of teaching."

Now Mrs. Bagnull did smile and leaned toward the teacher. "I'm so pleased we understand each other. Marvin tells me how thoroughly he enjoys school this year. He doesn't say a great deal—he's rather modest, you know—but he's constantly saying lovely things about you, even though, as I understand, you teach the lower grades...primarily." Her smile showed small, even teeth, with lips lightly covered with lipstick.

"Any teacher would be delighted to have Marvin as a pupil."

Quite relaxed now, Mrs. Bagnull took off her coat and revealed a dark blue silk dress with a large silver brooch pinned at the top. She lightly fingered the expensive accessory. "And then I planned this party for tonight. You know, to honor the winners of the essay contest. Since Marvin had already won two years in a row, naturally we expected him to win first place again. Not just me, you understand, but the entire North Prairie community. To hear differently, well, it will shock my friends—utterly shock them." She stopped fingering her ornament and smiled again. "You are a delightful person, Mrs. Bennett, and I hope you'll be at the party tonight."

"I am sorry, but I will not be able to attend tonight, Mrs. Bagnull."

"Please call me Marlene. I feel as though we will become good friends and I hope you won't mind if I call you Ophelia."

"I will not change the winner's list."

"I—I beg your pardon."

"Mrs. Bagnull—uh, Marlene—I did not decide on the winners. To reverse the decision would be dishonest and unfair. Frankly, Max wrote a better essay."

"A better essay? I doubt that."

"You misunderstand. Marvin *could* have written the best essay again, easily, but he was a little cocky and slightly careless. He spent too little time in preparing. Max, on the other hand, spent hours writing and rewriting. No, Marlene, I will not alter anything."

"I can't believe—" Her shocked expression reinforced her words. "But you said—"

"No, Marlene, *you* said!"

"Don't you realize what this means? Why, this could ruin Marvin's whole life! He *deserves* that award. You said yourself that he could do a better job than Max."

"I did not say he deserved it. Max deserved it because he earned it; Marvin could have earned it, but he did not. That is the difference."

"Surely you are not serious! You are new to North Prairie, my dear Ophelia, so you don't know about that—that boy. That Max Waxman. Do you really know him? He's stupid! He must have copied his essay or something."

"I am certain it is original."

"Everyone knows that he's stupid. Perhaps that's too strong a word. I don't know what's happened this year, but everyone knows he's, well, dull. And he's the son of a constantly drunk father, and he has no mother, and his poor aunt must work to pay her own bills and those of—"

"What does a drunken father and a hard-working aunt have to do with Max winning the contest?"

"Everything! Why, we can't have trash like that—"

"I think you have said enough, *Mrs.* Bagnull."

"On the contrary, Mrs. Bennett, I've not said nearly enough. I warn you, this is only the beginning—"

"Oh, I am sure of that," she said evenly.

"Mr. Bagnull is on the school board, you know, and—"

"And he's certainly free to bring this issue before the board. But I doubt that he would. Do you think he will choose to do that?"

"I didn't mean bring it before the board. I only wanted to remind you of his position. Contract renewal time comes up soon and matters such as pay increments and—"

"You have said enough. You cannot intimidate me. I have dealt with such difficult situations before. Right now, my concern is for Marvin."

"For Marvin? You don't act that way." Marlene's mouth opened in surprise. "He seems the last thing you care about—"

"My concern is that one day Marvin will be thankful I refused to give in to your demands. He needs to learn that his parents cannot buy or coerce people into giving him everything in life. He needs to *earn* it." She leaned forward, her face only inches from the woman. "He also needs to learn to fail. You have prevented his learning such a valuable lesson. That is, you have until now."

"Well, I never—" She grabbed her coat and swept from the room.

The door banged loudly behind her.

Mrs. Bennett chuckled as she heard the starter grinding several times before the engine roared.

For a long time afterward, she sat at her desk and stared into space. Then, looking down at her hands, she said aloud, "God, I've had four months with these pupils. Four nearly perfect months. They are the most promising class I have ever taught. Why must all this happen now? Will you not allow us to have peace—at least a little longer?"

Even as she asked, Ophelia Bennett knew the answer to her own prayer.

14

IF OPHELIA BENNETT EXPECTED A SUDDEN EXPLOSION OF ANGER, she was mistaken. The Bagnulls arranged the party for the winners of the essay contest. Miss Perkins hovered over the winners and frequently told them and their parents how proud she was.

The next morning Edwina Perkins told her that the Bagnulls had been extremely gracious to everyone. "I thought she'd be so upset that she'd cancel the party, but it was a great event, even better than last year. And Marlene makes the most delicious cakes in the entire community—especially her coconut."

On the surface, no trouble appeared. Ophelia Bennett knew, however, it was only a matter of time. "The undercurrent will build and erupt," she said to herself. "Not today, but soon."

*

At the end of the last school day before Christmas, Michael raised his hand. "Mrs. Bennett, my mother says I have to bring home school books to study during the vacation time. I told her I was caught up on everything, but I guess she didn't believe me. She said I couldn't come home tonight without books."

"I understand. Hmm. I suggest you take your arithmetic book—the third grade one—and do as many pages as you can on mixed fractions. You are a little weak there, and the extra study may help."

"Is that ever going to be boring!"

"Make a game out of it," Marvin said. "Try to beat yourself. Set a goal of ten problems in ten minutes. If they're too hard, give yourself two minutes apiece. Or maybe two pages each day and see if you can do more."

"That is quite a good idea," Mrs. Bennett said to Marvin. "You see, Michael, you can make up your own games. Make fun out of your arithmetic book. You do not have to depend on me to show you how...after all, I will not always be your teacher."

"But you're the best teacher in the whole world. I hated all the teachers until you came to North Prairie," Ginger said.

At that moment, Edwina Perkins came into hearing range. Her back was to Ginger, but Ophelia Bennett observed the flush at the back of her neck.

"Do not say—"

"You are the best! The very best!" called out Marvin.

"Please, this is not—"

"Mrs. Bennett," Ginger interrupted, "my father says I'd better bring home books too."

"All right, then do whatever he says."

"And, well, you might as well give us all books," Nickolas said. "That's what our parents have been saying and most of them have agreed that if we don't do that, they'll cause trouble for you."

"You weren't supposed to tell her. You promised," Ginger said.

"I'm sorry, but I'm mad."

"Nickolas should've said *angry*. To be mad means crazy." Stephen raced to the board.

"Well, anyway, I'm angry. We all talked and promised not to tell you, but I guess I did, so—"

"Okay, it's like this." Ginger sighed. "Our parents are getting so they spend almost the whole night talking. Most of us are on the same party line, so they don't have much trouble talking to each other. And it's mostly just Mrs. Bag—I mean, it's mostly only a couple of parents, but everyone listens in."

"That's right," Karen said. "They keep asking us what's going on here at our school. Every night at supper, my dad asks, 'And what kind of games did you play today?' For a while I kept trying to explain that we worked hard and learned, but he wouldn't listen. So now I just shut up and eat."

"Yeah!" Carol jumped to her feet. "Someone's been talking to our parents about our school. *Someone didn't keep our secret.* And we all promised!"

"I'll break his neck if I find out," Nickolas thundered, eyeing Marvin.

"Enough!" Mrs. Bennett called out and clapped her hands loudly. "If your parents want you to bring books home, that is exactly what you will do. All of you know the areas where you are weak. Do not take this as a dreaded duty, but you could make it a challenge for yourself. Do not feel resentful or angry, but determine to improve during this Christmas vacation."

"Yes, children," Edwina Perkins said. "Respect your parents' wishes."

"Max, your penmanship is still poor," Mrs. Bennett said. "Michael, you need additional work in phonics and more practice with your reading."

"Yvonne, work on English grammar," Miss Perkins said. "You are doing well enough, but you still have to think through each rule. Practice at home until you speak automatically. I know you can do it. You might even find a way to help us become more fluent in Spanish."

"And Larry, you need—"

"Mrs. Bennett, I'm sorry to interrupt, but you don't understand. Our parents have been talking about *you,*" Nickolas said. "All our parents...well, most all of them. They get on the phone or they go see each other and you're the one they talk about. Don't you care?"

"I care very much, and it is quite sad to me. And thank you for being so concerned. I do not believe I have done anything wrong. Some of your parents are angry, but it is because they do not understand."

"And they're so mean," Karen said.

"Do not think that way. They are confused and probably quite frightened that I am doing something harmful. When people do not understand, they often behave strangely. They have undoubtedly learned that I teach differently here. I can do nothing to change them. And so, because I cannot change them, I choose to do nothing."

"But aren't you mad? I mean, angry?" Nickolas asked.

"Why don't you stand up to them?" Carol asked.

"You said that just like Barbara Stanwyck did in *Banjo on My Knee,"* Karen said. "She raised her fist, like you did."

"I cannot work that way. Many years ago, my husband said, 'We cannot use the devil's tools to fight God's battles.' He meant that it is not right to do anything wrong, regardless of what others do. I believe in a God who helps us face whatever happens."

"You wouldn't be doing wrong to tell the truth," Max said.

"True, but I would have to speak against others. And I have also learned anger incites anger and each time harsh words spread, they grow stronger." She almost added, "And more violent."

"But you don't just let them do bad things, do you?" Max asked.

"I believe that God will give us strength to fight the battles that we need to fight. When we do not need to fight, He provides us with peace."

"Huh? I don't understand that," Michael said.

"She means that she prays and God lets her know what to do," Max said. "She has prayed and God hasn't told her to do anything."

"That is correct. This is the time for me to focus on you children and on your education. That is what I believe God has told me to do. Furthermore, I do not anticipate doing anything or saying anything to—"

"But they are saying dreadful things about you," Ginger said. "Mean, terrible—"

"Should I now say bad things about them? They are your parents and I respect them, and I know that even if they are mistaken or wrong, they love you and believe they are doing the best for you. Is that correct?"

"Sure, but still—" Nickolas said.

"I have God's peace in my heart. I believe that truth and right will triumph eventually. Perhaps not immediately, but always ultimately."

"But they've said horrible things. Exaggerations. Lies!" Ginger protested. "You can't let them say things like that without—"

"We do not fight our enemies by returning the wrongs they do to us. We may not like what they say or do. We may even feel sorry for them. I must not do a greater wrong in trying to correct the evils they bring about."

"I don't think that's fair!" mumbled Nickolas. "They're wrong."

"I hope you will always want good to triumph over wrong. You have a special spirit of caring about the underdog. Do not lose that. It is one of your great talents."

"I—I won't, ma'am."

"I'll stick up for you, Mrs. Bennett!" Marvin yelled, glaring at Nickolas. "I wouldn't ever do anything to hurt you. And I didn't blab about you either. So there!"

"And I wouldn't either, would I?" the perpetually questioning first grader said.

"I wouldn't either!" called out another voice.

As other students loudly vowed their loyalty, Ophelia Bennett held up her hand. "Stop! I know you mean it. Loyalty and love are two great things in the world. I shall always treasure this moment."

Later, after the children had gone, Edwina Perkins sat next to Mrs. Bennett's desk. "I've learned so much from you in these months here at North Prairie. You've made me into a good teacher."

"Thank you, but I can only work with a person who has something inside that is ready to receive help. You are an excellent teacher—an outstanding educator—and you will continue to grow. You simply needed someone to give you confidence and to draw you out. Do you realize how much of the teaching you have guided during the past month?"

"I had a good teacher."

"Perhaps, but you are now creating your own programs. You have invented several learning games. Edwina, you're a clever, original, and natural teacher. You will go a long way in the field of education if you stay with it."

"I owe everything to you," she said. "You taught me everything that teachers college didn't."

Mrs. Bennett squeezed the younger woman's hand. "Thank you."

"I owe you so much, Ophelia. And, like the pupils, I'll always be loyal to you. I hope you know that."

"Yes, my dear, I know you mean it." Ophelia Bennett closed her eyes and folded her hands in front of her. She repeated, almost inaudibly, "Yes, I know you mean it. At least, you mean it right now."

15

WHILE THE TWO TEACHERS SAT IN THE SCHOOL BUILDING, Marlene Bagnull finished her second cup of coffee with Gladys Whiting. "I think it's time we investigate what's going on at that school."

"And yet they seem to enjoy school. Karen's report card—"

"Don't be foolish. A teacher can write anything she wishes on a report card. Of course Karen likes school. So does Marvin. But that doesn't mean they're learning anything."

"Maybe, but..."

"And another thing. Have you noticed everything centers on Mrs. Bennett? She signed all the report cards. She's the one Marvin constantly talks about. But Edwina Perkins is their teacher, not Mrs. Bennett. Miss Perkins we know and respect. Have you compared the report grades with last year's?"

"I've thought about that."

"Why shouldn't Karen and Marvin and the others like Mrs. Bennett? She lets them play all the time. If you ask me, she's just taken over that school and allows them to do anything they please. They don't bring books home. I try to question my son about what they learned in school and he gives me vague answers."

"I suppose you're right," Gladys mused as she sipped her coffee. "Actually, I've suspected something for a long time. Karen used to bring home four or five books, and she always spent at least an hour working on them. I had to help her, of course, but now she doesn't bring anything home. Well, fiction stories—those dreary stories that no self-respecting child ought to read at that age. And some are *adult* fiction books. Why, she's currently reading *Jane Eyre*. That's not a fit story for a girl of her age. I simply don't understand."

"I know exactly what you mean. When I try to question Marvin, he always gives me vague answers. Something strange is going on at North Prairie School this year, if you ask me."

As Gladys Whiting listened, she decided that Marlene had verbalized an uneasy feeling she had pushed aside for weeks. Karen had not brought home her work in the evenings. Whenever she questioned her daughter, Karen always answered, "Oh, I finished everything at school." When asked about what she had studied or what class she had enjoyed, Karen always replied vaguely, "Oh, they're all good. We studied, you know, the usual things."

"Yes," Gladys said, "perhaps we ought to find out what is going on at North Prairie School."

"I've already spoken to three other parents and they are as upset as you are," Marlene said. "I am so glad you are expressing yourself so well. You have convinced me that we are doing the proper thing."

16

HEAVY SNOW BLANKETED THE NORTHERN PORTION OF ILLINOIS in early December. Three days of warmer weather followed and caused some melting, but by the time Christmas vacation arrived, the ground lay under a crust of two inches of ice. During the holiday period children crossed and crisscrossed the empty fields and roads, marring the soft-white covering.

Boy had played with the other children in his neighborhood every day. By the day after Christmas he had tired of sledding and skating. He had already made two snow forts and an igloo. He wanted to be back in school again.

"I don't want to build a fort again today," he told Max. He even turned down a chance to skate on the Harrison pond with Nickolas. He had completed all his schoolwork. Today reading bored him.

"I don't feel like playing with my toys," he had told his aunt. "I guess I'll go outside for a while." Without consciously considering his actions, Boy cut through the Bagnulls' back yard and trudged through snowdrifts up to his waist as he traveled cross country.

He stood at the road and stared ahead, especially where Mrs. Bennett parked her car. Since he had been there the day before, someone had shoveled the snow in front of North Prairie School.

He felt foolish coming to the empty school, yet he hoped that simply by being there, he might see Mrs. Bennett. She had not visited the school since vacation started—he had checked every morning and every afternoon. Besides, he would have known from the car tracks. No car had driven into the school driveway.

He walked slowly inside the fenced-in playground and up to the heavy door. He rattled the handle. Of course, it was locked. Boy moved away from the building. The sun had begun to melt the snow that morning and he could feel the slush under his boots. He had left home wearing mittens, but the day was already so warm he had put them in his pocket.

He stood at the side of the building, listening, as melting snow gently trickled down the drainpipe and across the front yard of the school. After several minutes, he brushed snow off one of the swings and pumped himself several times, but it was no fun swinging alone. He couldn't think of a game to play outside by himself. If Mrs. Bennett were here, she'd know what he could do. Still more than a week before the school vacation would be over.

He first saw the dark object while in the swing, but thought it was only a small limb previously broken off by heavy winds and covered by snow that was now showing through because of the melting temperatures. Boy looked again, but it didn't seem quite like wood. Slowly he got out of the swing, walked over, and started to kick the object with his boot.

It was a billfold, made of cow skin that had worn smooth on the outside. He picked it up and wondered who had dropped it. Inside he found two five-dollar bills and three ones. He also found a card showing the owner: *Ophelia Bennett, 1911 Galilee Avenue, Zion, Illinois.*

Boy wiped the billfold carefully and thrust it into an inside pocket and ran back home, retracing his steps. He felt winded, but exhilarated. Running next door, he told his aunt, "I'm going for a ride on my bike."

He didn't wait for a reply and raced away from the house. As long as he stayed on the main road, he would be fine.

Boy didn't stop to reason the wisdom of his plan. He knew only that he was going to see his teacher. The highway was cleared and he could follow Highway 173 on his bicycle all the way to Galilee Avenue. He guessed it was maybe five miles and that didn't seem such a long way to pedal. He didn't know exactly where 1911 Galilee was, but he knew that Highway 173 went right through Zion. All the streets going north and south had Bible names and those going east and west had numbers. If he remembered correctly, Galilee was right after the railroad viaduct. It wouldn't be difficult to find. By bicycle he could make the trip in no time.

Boy hadn't thought about the long hills. Just outside Zion, he encountered two hills that were too steep for him to pump on his bicycle, so he got off and pushed. By the time he got to the Zion city limits, the sun had already begun its descent. The bright glint of the sun's rays on the snow hurt his eyes. He had started to perspire, but he had learned not to loosen his heavy coat, although he did stuff his scarf into his pocket.

He finally reached the top of the hill. Imitating the yell of Tarzan in the movies, he first coasted and then pedaled rapidly downward.

It was nearly 3:30 when he spotted the railroad viaduct ahead. Through naked trees he saw Galilee Avenue. As he coasted down to Galilee, he hesitated about which direction to go. There were no houses on the right side, so he made a left turn. As he started up Galilee, he realized it wasn't paved and it had not been plowed. Some of the drifts were more than two feet high. He began to push his bike. As he pondered how far he would have to go, he spotted Mrs. Bennett's Ford in the driveway at the next house.

The car, covered with snow, was parked just barely in the driveway. From the looks of it, Boy figured the car hadn't been driven for days—at least not since the last snow.

He stopped next to her car, leaned his bike on the kickstand, and started toward the door. No one had shoveled the driveway. No footprints marred the five steps to the door or the small, unenclosed porch.

He knocked timidly and waited. His feet were cold and he felt quite tired. It had been a long ride—farther than he had anticipated.

The heavy door opened and Ophelia Bennett stood in front of him. Her surprise turned into a brilliant smile. "How very nice of you to visit. Come in, please." She stepped back for him to enter.

"Here," he said, handing her the billfold, "this was on the playground, over by where you park your car. I just found it this morning, so I got on my bike and came over as soon as I could."

"Thank you so much."

"I thought you might be worried."

"I was not worried, but I knew I did not have it. I missed it the first night after school was over. I thought I must have left it in my desk at the school. I am so pleased that you found it." She pointed to a chair. "Sit down. I'll make you a cup of Ovaltine. Is that all right?"

"Don't care," he said, but he felt as if she offered him a great gift.

"It will take only a few minutes." As she turned toward the kitchen, she added, "Just sit down and take off your boots."

Boy pulled off his heavy boots and propped them against the door on top of a small, braided rug. He plopped into a straight chair and looked around the room. It was narrow with polished hardwood under a large rug that went almost to the door. A sofa, three chairs, a large, filled bookcase, and an oil heater were the only objects in the room. No pictures hung on the walls. By leaning slightly forward, he could see into the dining room. A man sat at the table but did not look at him. Boy kept staring, but the man never seemed to move. Bored with watching him, Boy walked over to the bookcase and stared at the titles. He didn't recognize any of them. He decided they were college books of some kind.

Ophelia Bennett returned with a cup of Ovaltine and two oatmeal cookies. "Does your aunt know you have come this way? It's a long distance from North Prairie by bicycle. She must be worried."

Until that moment, he hadn't thought about his aunt. "Gosh, no, I didn't even think about her worrying. I—I just wanted to return this to you.

Thought you might need the money or something or—"

"Yes, thank you, but your aunt must be worried."

"Guess the billfold was all I thought about."

"I'll give her a ring on the telephone." Boy gave her the number and she went into the dining room. He heard Mrs. Bennett asking the operator to give her North Prairie 2104, his number. A minute later she returned and sat down, watching Boy as he finished his second cookie.

"Your aunt had begun to worry about you, because you did not come in for your lunch. It will be dark soon, and I told her that I would drive you home right away. She said to leave the bicycle, and your father will stop by tomorrow and put it into his truck."

"Yes'm. He comes to Zion regular like—I mean, regularly."

"Is that all right? Leaving your bicycle here? Your aunt said you could get along one day without it."

"Oh, oh, yes, ma'am, that is fine." Boy smiled. He hadn't anticipated that Mrs. Bennett would drive him back to North Prairie. Inside her car. With her. He felt warm and good. "I would appreciate that very much," he said in his most sophisticated voice.

*

As Boy finished the last sip of his Ovaltine, the man who sat in the dining room got out of his chair and walked slowly to the living room. He stood mutely in the doorway and his pale-blue eyes surveyed the room. "Hello, Mr. Bennett."

The man's eyes appeared vacant and he said nothing. He was tall, gray-haired, and thin. His face seemed old and Boy noticed white whiskers he had missed while shaving. He sat on the sofa facing the boy.

"Uh, my name is Boy Masters, sir." He extended his hand.

Woodenly, the man took his hand and, although limp, Boy shook it.

Calmly Mrs. Bennett said, "This is my husband, Richard Bennett. He has been ill a long time. He hears everything you say but does not speak."

"What's wrong with him?"

"He was in a kind of—accident a long time ago."

"And he's been like that since then? Will he get better?"

"I do not know, although it is not likely. He is alive and I am thankful for that. You see, part of the trouble is that his brain has been damaged and he does not remember most things. One of the things he cannot remember is how to speak."

"How did it happen? I mean, what kind of accident?"

She stared at Boy but said nothing.

"If I shouldn't have asked, I'm sorry."

"No, that is not why I hesitate. After all, have I not told you often enough to ask questions when you do not understand? If I did not wish to discuss it, I would have told you so. Never be satisfied with answers unless the answers satisfy you. Ask questions. Find out."

"So, uh, what's wrong?"

"I am not certain how much to tell you, which is why I hesitated. It is such a long story." She laughed self-consciously and then took several deep breaths. Pulling a chair two feet in front of him, she sat down. "When I first came to North Prairie School, we said the way we studied would be our secret. Do you remember that?"

He nodded and raised his cup for another swallow of Ovaltine, only to realize his cup was empty.

"This is another secret. If you want to know, I shall tell you, but it is not for you to repeat. This is a secret between you and me. Is that understandable?"

"Oh, I won't tell, Mrs. Bennett. I promise. It'll be our secret. Honest."

17

OPHELIA BENNETT TOLD BOY MASTERS what happened that Thursday, January 22, 1933. She would never forget that night as long as she had breath in her.

*

In Benson, at the southern tip of Lake County, life had been hard for many years. From the beginning of 1929, conditions worsened. Banks failed and so did crops. Factories closed or laid off large numbers of employees. Larger cities set up food lines. By 1933, the newly inaugurated president, Franklin D. Roosevelt, had begun a public works program that employed many of the husbands and fathers. They planted trees, improved highways, and cleared swamps.

Richard and Ophelia Bennett had been luckier than most. They both taught in the Woodrow Wilson Elementary School. Four teachers had taught there in 1929; three remained the following year. In 1931, the school board had kept only the Bennetts—with a contract for half of their former salaries. As it was, they didn't receive any money anyway. The school board issued what they called scrip, but at least they could trade the paper for food and clothes in the local stores.

Benson had one colored elementary school less than a mile from Woodrow Wilson School. By Christmas the single teacher and his twelve students heard the solemn word: No more funds. No money for the teacher, no money to operate, to heat, to buy paper, books, or kerosene for the lamps.

When Richard heard that the county had closed the school, he took the initiative and invited the twelve children into the Woodrow Wilson School. Because the colored children sat in the back of the classroom, and the Bennetts asked for no additional income, no one seriously objected. Two white parents protested to the school board, but when assured that their own children would not suffer, they accepted the fact.

"Shucks, guess it won't hurt so long's they stay in the back and keep to themselves and don't stop our kids from learning," one board member said, commenting on the hundreds of dollars the Bennetts had saved the school system.

But the Negro children had not remained in the back of the room after the first week. Not because they forced their way to the front, but the Bennetts encouraged them to mix with the others. "God created all people. We have our skin differences, but I do not believe God cares about that," Ophelia said when one of the white children objected. "And you can learn so much from each other's backgrounds."

"God is color blind," Richard said regularly and smiled at the children. He said it to the colored children as often as he did to the white.

One morning Ophelia moved James Jones, a bright second grader and a Negro, to the front row. "James's eyes are too bad to sit anywhere else," she explained. "Just because he cannot see the blackboard from the back should not stop him from learning like the rest of you."

None of the white children said anything. None of them spoke to James either. At recess time, as they passed by his desk, two of the boys punched James on the back of the head. On the playground, another tripped him and one boy would have knocked him down if he hadn't spotted Mr. Bennett watching.

When they came inside after recess, James raised his hand. "Mr. Bennett, sir, I'd like to have another seat. You know, in the back of the room."

"Why would you want that?"

" 'Cuz I can see all right somewhere else," he said and lowered his head.

"You will stay where you are."

"But Mr. Bennett, sir—"

Richard Bennett faced the children and allowed his gaze to shift from face to face. "Do any of you have a problem with James sitting here? If his parents had money for glasses, I would agree for him to sit elsewhere. But his parents are as poor as the rest of you. No, they are even poorer."

"Maybe they're lazy," Torry Martin said and laughed. He was the tallest white boy in the school. "I heard all niggers are lazy."

"It is quite easy to call people lazy when they do not work because others will not give them the opportunity," Mr. Bennett said and stood in front of Torry. "It is the way many people justify such injustice."

"That's not what my daddy says," Torry persisted.

"We are not here to discuss your father's opinion or his prejudice." He stared into the eyes of the boy. "We are here to learn. In this classroom, everyone has an equal opportunity to learn. Do you agree that giving everyone a chance is a good idea?"

"Yeah, guess so."

"Excellent. Then this topic is closed!"

A few grumblings and undertones came from two white boys, but no one said anything distinctive enough for Richard Bennett to understand.

*

As the three-quarter moon slid toward one side of the sky, it remained high enough to shed a pale, wintry glow. Thin, wispy clouds crossed in front of the moon and painted their lacy edges against purest silver.

It should have been a normal winter night. Just then, a rock through the window shattered the quietness. Shards of glass splayed the bedroom of the Bennetts's single-story house. Wild cheering followed.

"God, help us!" a frightened Ophelia screamed. The rock had missed her head by inches. Her hands shook as she picked up the stone, the size of a large grapefruit.

Richard sat up. "What is going on?" He jumped out of bed and pulled his trousers over his nightshirt.

By now, Ophelia had leaped from the bed and pulled on the long string hanging in the middle of the room. Immediately light chased out the darkness. She stifled a gasp as she stared at the broken glass and the stone.

"The cowards!" Richard muttered as he hurriedly buttoned his trousers.

From the opposite side of the room, a thunderous crack pierced their ears and pieces of glass struck their armoire. Tiny particles of glass covered the floor. Richard put on his high-top shoes without lacing them. He started across the room and stopped when he saw the piece of paper tied to the rock.

Ophelia also saw the second rock and picked it up. She unfolded the paper and stared at the single sentence: *GET RID OF THE NIGGERS.*

"Stay here," he said. "I am going outside to face them."

"Richard!" she called and stopped. Richard would face them and no one would make him run, she knew, no matter how many people waited outside.

Over her woolen nightgown, she slipped on her heavy housecoat. She gave no thought to her long, unbound hair and followed a few feet behind him.

The Bennetts had never locked their doors. Richard turned the handle, threw open the door with boldness, and stepped outside. He stood on the porch.

Figures scurried away or hid behind trees.

"I received your message!" Richard shouted. "Are you afraid to face me? Afraid to speak up and show me who you are?"

A cold wind sprang out of nowhere and caused the two pine trees to sway as if they responded to music. Threatening clouds inched their way across the horizon.

"I am not afraid of you! You sneak up at night. You are cowards—every one of you. Why will you not show yourselves? Talk to me like men!" He waited on the porch but no one moved. Yet he knew several of them remained hidden.

So, they had not expected him to face them. Most of their victims probably cowered behind closed doors.

Ophelia, meanwhile, had lit a hurricane lantern and brought it to the porch. She stood beside her husband.

"Yes, you see we are willing to stand in the light!" he yelled. "Why are you hiding in darkness?"

Ophelia's free hand clasped his.

"Just as I thought. You will not come to the light because you prefer to hide in darkness."

"You do not frighten me either!" she yelled. "You are cowards! All of you!"

"When you can build up enough courage, we welcome you to come back and speak to us—face to face."

He took his wife's hand and they went back inside the house.

*

The next morning, after they had boarded up both windows, the Bennetts arrived at school. When Richard started to unlock the door, he saw the paper. Someone had wedged a sheet of school-lined paper into a crack.

Both of them knew the intent, if not the actual words, before Richard had unfolded the single sheet. Scrawled in awkwardly printed capital letters was the second message: *WE KILL NIGGER LOVERS.*

Richard stared at it several seconds and then his eyes searched his wife's face.

Understanding his unspoken question, she said, "We have done the right thing. We will not back down or run from them."

"I have to be sure before we go any further." He held the paper in his hands. "They are serious. I have no idea what will happen, and I am not sure to what lengths—"

"I will take care of this!" She grabbed the paper out of his hand and wadded it into a ball. "Some of the parents need penmanship classes worse than their children." She forced herself to laugh. "Perhaps we are teaching the wrong people."

"You do not have to fight this," he said quietly. "I was the one who asked the colored children to come because I believe in equality—"

"Hmmm, and I am your wife, which means that we are in this together. Besides, I would have spoken up if you had not."

"Yes, I know that. It is only—"

"That now you know it will get worse. You did not know the vehemence when we started, didn't you?"

"I knew."

"So are you afraid for me? Is that it?"

This time he only nodded.

"This is my choice as well."

"But it may get worse—"

"May get worse? Of course it will get worse."

"We may have to stand up against all the whites in the community. I am not trying to start a crusade or—"

"This is our decision—mine as much as yours."

Richard Bennett embraced his wife and kissed her. It was something he had never done before in a public place. This time they did not care if he defied tradition. Ophelia knew it was a special moment of their silent-but-committed unity.

They never talked about their activities with the colored children again. They had made their commitment. They would stick with it.

Even if they had not been threatened, the Bennetts felt the hostile attitude of other whites toward them every time they were in public. None of the stores refused them service, but other customers who came in after them frequently had their orders filled first. Their mail delivery ran three or four days late. When they approached a group of people in the park or on the street, as soon as they were noticed, the group hurriedly disbanded. Individuals walked past them, and no one spoke to them in public. In fact, it was almost as if the citizens had conspired together—and the Bennetts sometimes speculated about whether there had been such a conspiracy—not one person acknowledged them in public except in direct answer to a question.

"Ever notice that even when they answer, no one ever smiles at us?" Richard asked.

"Smile? They cannot even look us in the eye," Ophelia said.

The reaction at church hurt them even more. Richard had been an usher, but that ended when they walked in to church one Sunday morning.

"We have so many ushers now," the pastor said when he met them at the door. "We don't need you to volunteer for the time being."

"I understand," Richard said, "but I wish you had had the courage to tell me the truth." He picked up a bulletin and sat next to his wife.

Minutes later, the pastor's wife, who was also the Sunday school superintendent, came to the pew where they sat. "Dear Ophelia, I'm sorry to tell you, but—"

"Stop, please," Ophelia said. "You no longer want me to teach the women's Sunday school class, is that correct?"

"Uh, well, uh—"

"I do not care what excuse you choose—that you have decided to combine the class or they need a new teacher. I understand. You could hardly punish Richard for acting like a true Christian and ignore me. I am honored to be dismissed for—"

"Why, that's a terrible thing to say—"

"But true," Ophelia said. "Please do not insult either of us by lying or trying to make it sound as if you are being honorable. Judas kissed Jesus, but it was still betrayal, was it not?"

"How dare—"

Richard stood. "It is settled. You do not want us to be actively identified with the church. Would you prefer that we stop attending?"

"I wouldn't ask—"

"Would you rather we not attend?" Ophelia stood next to her husband.

"I do think that might be a good idea. For a time."

Ophelia raised her hand as if she were speaking to one of her pupils. "You need say no more." She moved out of the aisle and handed the pastor's wife her bulletin. "You might be able to use this."

They left the church where they had been actively involved and attended services at the largest church in the city. They sat in their car until the church bell chimed 11:00. They sat in the last row and left as soon as the pastor began the benediction.

Richard never spoke against anyone, not even against those at his church. Twice Ophelia started to spew out anger, but he stopped her. "Jesus said that his killers didn't know what they were doing. The white people are not mean, but they are afraid. We have to learn to love them, regardless of what they do."

*

It took another week before the tenseness permeated the classroom. The coloreds and the whites ignored each other. No one said a word to any child from the other group. None of the students looked directly at each other. Each tried to appear as if the other group was invisible.

Each night, Ophelia lay in bed with silent tears on her face.

*

The children know something terrible is building in the community, Ophelia thought. *White or colored. Does not matter. They all know that something is going to happen and that it will take place soon.* Despite the coal stove that warmed the large classroom, Ophelia felt sheathed in cold sweat. Throughout the day, when she thought about the children, her chest tightened and she was able to draw breath only with effort.

She looked across the room at her husband, down on his haunches with first and second graders. He laughed with that rich, baritone voice she loved to hear. It was only when she peered into his eyes that she knew he too waited.

Turning around as if staring out the window, she took six slow, deep breaths. *I must be strong. I must be strong. Oh, God, give me the strength I need to be strong for what lies ahead. Make me as strong as Richard.*

18

ON TUESDAY, JANUARY 20, all the children seemed tense and restless, especially the white children. Whenever there was an unexpected noise, at least one child was startled and others would turn their gaze toward the door.

Richard and Ophelia said nothing to each other. Their gaze met midmorning; he nodded and called the children to put away their books. "I'm going to teach you to play spelling baseball," he said.

Children from all eight grades, blacks and whites, were mixed on the two teams. As a batter received a turn, Richard pitched a word. Students received only words they were expected to know for their grade level. A student could request a word from the next higher grade level and, if successful, score a home run. Otherwise, each correctly spelled word counted for a one-base hit. It took four correctly spelled words to count for one run.

If bases were loaded (that is, if three preceding students had spelled a word correctly), and the next in line asked for a word on the next grade level and spelled it correctly, all four received a run. However, if the word asked for was misspelled, it counted for two outs instead of one for a single misspelled word.

The game had gone well and the competition was keen. The children who were not currently "at bat" kept score. After two innings, Richard appointed captains who pitched words to the opposing team.

The score was tied and two were on bases at the bottom of the sixth inning. There had been two outs before Lester Stobbe came to bat.

"Give me a fourth-grade word," the young boy, a third grader said. "I think our team can win this one."

Donald Otis, the leader of the opposing team, grinned and looked carefully over the fourth-grade words, trying to select what he felt was the most difficult one. "Okay, here it is. Spell *deceive*."

Lester grinned and winked at Mr. Bennett. "Deceive. D-e-c-e-i-v-e. Deceive."

And the shouting began. The Flash Gordon team had beaten Dick Tracy's. But the Dick Tracy people did not take it well. "That's not fair!" screamed William Myers.

"Yeah, he knew Donald was going to ask that word!" yelled one boy.

"Those niggers shouldn't be in our school anyway!"

"That's right. That's what my daddy says!" backed up another Dick Tracy member.

"Enough! I am disappointed in the Dick Tracy team. You lost, and you played a good game." Richard Bennett's pale-blue eyes flashed. "Do not spoil it now by getting angry and saying things you will later regret."

Even as he spoke, Ophelia knew his words came too late. This would be the end of everything. Children would tell parents and there would be more broken windows and threatening notes. Or worse.

For several seconds, no one spoke. The Dick Tracy team glared at the Flash Gordon players. Richard stood helplessly, his gaze switching from face to face.

Ophelia had never seen such hardness—such undisguised hostility—in the eyes of the children. No one needed to explain. They too had become part of the growing conspiracy, because they had innocently sided with their parents.

"I think we need a recess period," she said. As soon as the children started to leave, she went to her husband and squeezed his arm in a silent, reassuring gesture.

"What next?" he asked in confusion.

She shook her head. "These children. These poor children are so filled with hatred. How can parents teach them to despise others?"

"Because they are afraid," he said. "We must not forget that. Fear does strange things to people. One of the worst is that they have to convince themselves that they are right, that we are wrong, and thus we have become the enemy."

"If only they could understand. If only we could explain, or talk to them or show—"

"They will not listen to us. It's too late."

"I know," she said, unable to hide her own despair.

"It will end soon, because it cannot go on much longer," he said hoarsely. "God is with us. Remember that."

"It is only that...sometimes I want to run away, to forget all this. I wish I could teach where people love each other."

He turned her around and laid his arms on her shoulders. "That will never be the case with you and me. As long as we are teachers, we will stir up controversy. I wish it were different. Oh, darling, especially for you, I wish it were different. You know, different so that we could live a normal life."

"I understand how it must be for us." She put her fingers to his lips. "You do not have to try to spare me or try to protect me. There is also that weak side of me—the part that wants to run away, the part that argues that we ought to resign and leave."

He kissed her fingertips. "We cannot do that."

"I know that, but sometimes—"

"If we leave, it will only make it easier for their hatred to spill over the next time anyone tries to make changes. No, we have to stay. God is with us."

"That is the secret of our strength. God *is* with us." She stared into his blue eyes and saw peace reflected. "You are the best man I have ever known. And we are doing the right thing. I know, even though I have occasional doubts."

Ophelia walked to the door of the school and stared at the children. None of them played. Like two armies prepared for war, they stood in separate groups and glared at each other. No one spoke words, but the hatred seethed in their eyes and in the tenseness of their muscles.

She wanted to pray, to ask for divine intervention, but no words came to her. A cold, blustery wind roared across the open field next to the school. Snow flurries drifted lazily downward. When Richard went outside, the children ran across the playground—the whites on one side and coloreds on the other—shouting and delighting in the snow.

After the children came back inside, the flurries increased and within an hour, a coat of white had painted the landscape. By early afternoon wind whined in the branches of the trees and the wet, heavy snow bent their branches earthward.

Ophelia shivered, not from the cold as much as from a premonition of what was coming next.

*

The climax arrived at afternoon recess. Both groups raced to the playground and began to build a snowman—one side determined to make one larger than the other.

Ophelia and Richard stood near the school door and watched. The laughs and shouts of the children lifted their spirits.

Then they heard Donald's voice. "You can't make a *snow*man!"

"We can and ours is bigger'n yours!" Lester yelled and stepped toward the larger white boy.

"You can't, 'cuz you're black and snowmen are only for whites! See, that's why snow is white and not black. It's reserved for us." By now, Donald was less than a foot from the boy he had taunted.

Before Richard could run to them, Donald slammed his fist into Lester's face and the colored boy responded with several strong punches to the boy's stomach. Lester fell to his knees and remained there coughing. One of the other boys started forward.

"Enough! No fighting in this school!" Richard shouted.

"Yeah, you have to protect those dirty niggers, don't you?" Donald screamed.

"I can lick that colorless thing!" Lester shouted.

Richard grabbed an arm of each boy and brought them together. "This is not the way we behave. Do you understand?"

"He started it!" Lester said.

"Did not! You kept yelling that I was—"

"Stop it! Both of you. The fight is over. Now shake hands and we shall go back inside."

"Ain't gonna shake his hand," Donald said.

"I just defended myself," Lester said.

"You will shake hands or I shall personally knock both of you off your feet."

Ophelia, now standing near the boys, saw the anger blaze in her husband's eyes.

"Now!"

Both kept their heads down. They did shake, but they turned their faces from each other. Richard placed an arm on the shoulder of each. "Now we go inside." The fingers on the top of their shoulder blades made both boys wince, but they went forward.

Ophelia started to walk back toward the school building.

"My old man will get you for this."

Ophelia didn't recognize which of the white boys spoke, but she had no doubt about the seriousness of the threat.

Her throat dried and she swallowed several times to moisten it. For a few seconds, she couldn't get her breath; each inhalation was shaken out of her before she could draw it all the way into her lungs.

19

"DO YOU THINK IT IS OVER?" RICHARD ASKED, trying to hide the tenseness in his voice. On Wednesday, the day after the altercation in the classroom and schoolyard, the children seemed quieter and spoke less among themselves.

"I hope so. The children seem calmer. Yes, perhaps it is over," she said, but as she mouthed the words, she didn't believe them. Richard had not heard the threat on the playground.

On the second day, it seemed like the old class again.

Yet something about the way the white children acted caused Ophelia to doubt. *It's like the calm right before the storm hits,* she thought.

*

At first, Ophelia thought it was only the howling wind, roaring around the small wooden frame house. But as she lay in the cold, dark room, she knew it was not wind. She distinctly heard the sound of feet—many feet crunching in the snow. Like the marching of an army around the house.

They were coming.

No hurling stones and no broken glass. This time they heard the rising voices singing "Onward, Christian Soldiers." It was obvious they had surrounded the house.

"Lord, God," she cried out. Grabbing for Richard's hand, she shook it. "They are here!"

Richard leaped from the bed and pulled his pants up over his nightshirt. "Stay in here. No matter what happens, don't leave this room until everything has quieted down." He slipped his shoes on without tying them and hurried into the living room.

Ophelia, refusing to stay in the bedroom, had her robe on before she peered out the window. This time, a row of figures, most of them wearing white, made a line that stretched around the entire house. They pounded a large cross in the front yard and someone poured kerosene over it and another person lit it.

Before she could reach the front door, the flames brightened and cast a glow over the front of the house.

Richard opened the door a split-second before the band of marchers came toward the porch. He threw the door open and stood in the doorway. Cold air rushed into the house.

Most of the visitors wore white sheets wrapped around their bodies; some wore masks. A few women stood beside their men with their bonnets pulled down to hide their features. Two of the white-robed men carried torches. Most of them carried clubs or boards with one hand and hurricane lanterns with the other.

"We've warned you again and again, Bennett, but you wouldn't listen!" shouted one man as he stepped forward. "We won't have them niggers in our school! You're ruining everything there."

Another voice thundered, "Will you get rid of those colored kids, Bennett?"

"As long as I remain at Wilson Elementary, every child is welcome, colored or white. To me, color makes no difference! And I shall tell you something else: Color makes no difference to God!"

Someone cursed him.

A woman threw a handful of stones that missed him.

"See? I told you he'd act like that!" a voice yelled as the man ran forward, grabbed Richard by the collar with his left hand, and punched him in the stomach with his right. The air knocked out of his body, Richard grabbed his stomach and tried to steady himself. A second punch on the top of his head forced him to fall forward, face down. A second man swung at his prostrate body with a club. Someone kicked his head repeatedly.

"Will you leave those coloreds alone?"

Richard shook his head.

"Hit him again, boys!" called a woman's voice. "Hit him real good until you knock some sense into that hard head of his."

Three more men joined the battering group and a barrage of blows hit the non-resisting body.

"You cowards!" Ophelia screamed, breaking through the group in the doorway. "You bring a whole army to attack one man!" She grabbed a broom and knocked one man away from her husband. She struck two others.

From behind her, someone grabbed her and pinned her arms. A second person forced the broom from her hands.

"Wildcat, ain't you?" yelled the man who held her.

"And you are a coward. I know who you are! I recognize your voice. You are Donald Otis's father." She kicked at his legs. "Fine example you are setting for your son."

"Just shut your mouth!"

She didn't feel the blow as pain, only as impact. One of the women rushed forward and kicked her shins.

"Get back!" cried the man who held her. "I'll handle this one." Momentarily he loosened his grip. Ophelia whirled and clawed at his masked face. In her frenzied anger, she had no idea of the deep scratches she was making or that she had done permanent injury to his right eye.

His scream of pain filled the air as he threw his weight against her. She felt herself reeling backward and only the porch railing broke her fall. She winced, and then screamed. "You, you evil—"

The woman who had kicked her shins weighed at least a hundred pounds more than Ophelia. She grabbed Ophelia's long hair and twisted her around. Unable to stop the momentum, the teacher fell on her back.

"You jest lay right there!" the woman yelled. "You move jest one inch and I'll break both o' yer legs!"

In too much pain to resist, Ophelia lay there, staring up at the woman, willing strength to flow through her body. "Oh, God, please—"

"Don't you be prayin' ta God. God hates what yer doing and yer gettin' punished fer it!" The woman punched her in the stomach.

Ophelia felt a blackness coming over her and she resisted. Her eyes fluttered and she fought to stay conscious. Lights and shadows filled her eyes, and then she stopped fighting.

"Let's go, boys. Maybe this time he's learned a lesson."

This time, through a blur, Ophelia recognized the voice of Torry Martin's father.

"Maybe this time he'll learn to do what's right." That was Jack Cavanaugh's father speaking.

"If not, the next time he jest may be real sorry!" yelled the woman who had knocked Ophelia to the ground.

"The next time'll be too late!" another voice said.

Several people laughed.

And the hooded marchers walked away.

Ophelia slowly pulled herself up to a sitting position. Tears of physical pain streaked her eyes. Helplessly, she watched them march down the street. They sang "Onward, Christian Soldiers" as they waved their clubs and held their lanterns high. Richard lay at least four feet away. Ophelia fell forward and crawled to his inert body. She shook him several times, but he did not respond. She didn't realize she had been holding her breath until she felt his pulse. Forcing herself to remain calm, she inhaled and exhaled slowly and deeply. "You are alive, darling," she said. "Do not give up, do not give up! We will win!"

*

The first streaks of dawn filled the horizon before Ophelia felt strong enough to attempt to lift her husband, and then she couldn't. Too heavy with his dead weight, she finally grabbed him by the shoulders and dragged him toward the door. She wanted to cry for help but realized how useless it would be. No one would come to her aid.

She finally dragged his entire body inside the house. As she reached for a match to light the lamp, her fingers tingled. The gnawing wind had frostbitten her fingers, but she had been unaware of it until now. It took her three matches before the odor of kerosene filled the room.

She pumped water from the kitchen sink into a large washbasin and grabbed a handful of dishtowels. Kneeling beside her husband, she started to cradle his head but recognized it was the source of his worst injuries. Blood flowed from a large gash along his forehead. Another one—later she realized it was the deepest—came from the top of his skull. And the third was from his shattered left cheekbone.

"Richard, Richard. Please, please speak to me," she pleaded as she gently wiped at the blood. She left him only one time…to grab and tear a sheet into strips to bind his wounds.

Richard opened his eyes and his eyelids fluttered. He smiled. "Love you...God loves us...love..." And he lapsed into unconsciousness.

They had no telephone, so she wrapped two blankets around him. She threw a coat over her nightgown and ran the four blocks to the doctor's house.

20

"SO YOU SEE, BOY, MY HUSBAND'S BRAIN WAS PERMANENTLY DAMAGED," Ophelia Bennett said. "He will never speak again or behave normally."

The boy stared at Richard a long time and tried to imagine what it must be like. In his mind, he could picture the hooded men. He had seen pictures of them in the newsreels at the movies. "I hate people like that!" He looked down, surprised to see that he had doubled his fists.

"You must not—no, you must not—allow such feelings to fill your heart. If you do, you are no better than they are."

"Don't you hate those people for what they did?"

"Hate them? No, there is no place in my heart for such feelings. At least not now. I suppose I did feel that way—at first. But I soon learned something quite important about life."

"What was that?"

"It took nearly a month before we knew Richard's condition would be permanent. A doctor from Chicago drove down to examine him."

She reached over and clasped her husband's hand. The first lines of a smile creased his face.

"I thought about Jesus quite often and, of course, others such as Paul and Peter. They all did the right things simply because they were the right things to do." She laughed self-consciously. "Does that sound too simple?"

Boy shook his head. "I'm not sure. I'll need to think on that some."

"I also knew that if I tried to hurt them or get even, it would be wrong for me. I would have no peace. I could have tried to get them imprisoned or fined." She shrugged. "It would not have brought back Richard's mind, would it?"

"No, ma'am. Still I think I'd want to do something!"

"For almost a month I felt that way. But I prayed and read my Bible and hardly talked to anyone." She paused and smiled as she pictured herself sitting for hours at Richard's bedside. "When you are alone and there is no one else, you turn to God. Or at least I did."

"And that helped, did it?"

"Oh, yes. You see, when people are frightened, they often do stupid things. No one intended to harm him this badly. I felt bitter. Angry. I was also angry with God for allowing them to do that. But, eventually, I gave in. God could have stopped the angry mob from killing Jesus, you know, but He did not. He had a higher, grander purpose, so Jesus died."

"And—and you forgave them?"

"Yes. I had no idea of any purpose of God in what happened, but I knew I could not be at peace until I learned to forgive. When the evil men killed Jesus Christ, He said He forgave them because they did not know what they were doing." With her free hand she clasped Boy's. "You see, unless we want to become sad, tormented people, we have to learn to forgive."

"Yes'm, I guess." He smiled. "But I'm terribly sorry, Mrs. Bennett. Honest."

Ophelia Bennett kissed Boy on the cheek. "I hope you will always be tender. I teach you reading and arithmetic, but I hope that as long as I am your teacher, you will learn other things, even more important things. Then, when I am—when I am no longer your teacher—"

"Don't say that. You're the best teacher in the world and I want you to stay as long as I'm in school. Please!"

Ophelia sighed. "Boy, if only your wishes could make life happen that way."

21

THE TWILIGHT HAD BEGUN TO LOSE ITS GRIP ON THE LAND. The sun cast gold and copper light as its final message for the night. It had been extremely warm for that time of year and the air hung motionless.

Twenty-three of the invited parents from North Prairie School arrived before dark at the Bagnull home. Most of them had walked, some by cutting across the pastures, and others followed the narrow, dirt driveway, which was only a quarter-mile from the paved road.

They squeezed into the Bagnulls' living room, and because they did not have enough chairs, the men stood against the wall or sat on the floor. Several parents attempted small talk, but the conversation had a subdued ring to it.

Marlene and Marvin Bagnull Sr. had debated at length over which parents to invite. They had immediately eliminated Max Waxman's aunt and the Ortega family and later a few others such as Ralph Harrison. He had spoken up in defense of Ophelia Bennett when Marlene had talked with him earlier in the week.

Marlene's lips smiled, but her eyes remained flat. She gazed from face to face, mentally going down her list. "I am delighted that everyone is here. Awfully nice of you to come over this evening. Let's get down to business right away." She nodded to her husband as she sat down next to Mrs. Hege.

Marvin Bagnull Sr. stood. "I don't want to waste any time. We called you here tonight because we're concerned about our children and our school. We don't know what goes on at North Prairie School this year. It really disturbs us."

"We've had trouble before," Catherine Murphy's father said. "I don't imagine this is any worse. Might not even be as serious. Why, do you remember when Catherine was in second grade and—"

"Yes, yes," Mr. Bagnull cut in, "we've had trouble before. We've had to force teachers to resign and—"

"And remember 'bout eight years ago when we men had to take turns coming to school every day because the older boys threatened to beat up that old Miss—uh—"

"Tucker," his wife said.

Rotund Phillip Whiting guffawed as he relived the incident. "And you know how scared she was. One day she made me come inside and sit in the back of the room." He started laughing. "And somebody threw a lighted firecracker at her and she jumped so high, she was on top of her desk before we knew it."

"I remember the time, too, when—" another voice interjected.

"Excuse me, everyone!" Marlene yelled. "Excuse me!" Standing, she said, "We all have many memories of the past. But I think we need to remain on the subject. Darling, if you'll carry on, Mrs. Whiting and I will serve coffee to everyone."

A dead silence filled the room.

"I don't intend to be rude," Marlene added, "but we can easily sidetrack ourselves and forget the purpose for our coming together, can't we?" She bestowed her widest smile on everyone.

"You're right, Marlene," Larry Leech's mother said.

"We've had difficulties in the past—many of them. Kids will be kids. Yes, they played a few tricks, caused a fracas or two, but we always managed to work things out, even if it took drastic measures. But this is different." She scanned the room. "Instead of our children tormenting and frightening teachers, this—this ogre has everyone afraid of her."

"Must be something like that. The school year's half over and we haven't had one complaint. Never been like this before," Phillip Whiting said.

"I don't know what's going on. I've asked Mrs. Bennett. At the last PTA meeting I talked to her quite awhile. As chairman of the school board I told her I needed to know of any problems. She looked at me with a blank expression and said, 'Why, Mr. Bagnull, we have no problems here. We can always use more supplies, especially reading books. But no problems with the children—not a single one.' So if you listen to the way she tells it, they're all a bunch of angels."

"And yet," Mrs. Whiting said as she paused from pouring coffee, "Karen doesn't bring school books home—unless we demand them. Now what kind of school is that?"

"I'm sure that no real learning is taking place this year," Marlene said. "After all, we all know our Marvin is extremely bright and—and, of course, so are many of your children. But when really stupid children such as Max Waxman or that Mexican child can win prizes over our children...it seems that something has to change."

"I suspicion there's some cheating going on," one parent said.

"Like she just marks on their report cards the kind of grades she wants," Mrs. Hege said. "I mean, how else do you explain that stupid boy and that

Mexican—"

"You know, I've been wondering about that myself," Beth Watkins said. "With my husband dead and my having to work all the time, I can't watch James and little Ralph the way I'd like. But they've always brought schoolbooks home and I've had to force them to get it done. However, none of that's been going on this year. Whenever I ask them anything, they shut up like clams. Or they'll say things such as, 'We like school. We really do.' Believe me, when my boys like school, something is very, very wrong."

"I think she lets them play all the time," Gerald Jenkins's father added.

"Perhaps we ought to insist that Miss Perkins become the principal next year the way she was last year. She got after those kids and didn't take any nonsense out of them," Mrs. Hege said. "She called me every time my boys got out of hand. I had to take off work twice last year to go to school. The first time was in early October and—"

"Yes, precisely! But let's not dwell on particulars right now," Marlene said as she patted Cecile Hege's shoulder. "I'm sure all of us could find many good things to say about Miss Perkins. Unfortunately, she is not our subject."

"If she were the principal there, things would be like they used to be!" Phillip Whiting pounded the arm of the rocker where he sat.

"That may be one step we'll have to consider—urging Mr. Pettygill to reinstate Miss Perkins next year. Since Mrs. Bennett has more years of teaching experience, she received the position."

"But she's also moved around a lot, hasn't she?" Helena Osborn asked. "My little Susan is only in first grade, but I've tried to look ahead. I'm not sure I want her to teach my little girl year after year. If a teacher is any good, I would think she'd stay in one place and become a significant influence in the community. But look at her record. This is at least her fourth school—"

"It's her sixth," Mr. Bagnull said. "And I've already checked into her background." He eyed the others. "Surely, we want stable, reliable teachers. I mean, she could even be a—a criminal."

"Is she? Is she a criminal?" Catherine Murphy's father asked.

"Well, not that. But she's been in trouble with parents and school boards before," Marlene said. "We should have looked into this before she came here. We didn't have to take her as our teacher. We could have fought Mr. Pettygill on this."

"And he listens when parents get together and make a lot of noise," Mr. Hege said quietly. "If we demand a change, Mr. Pettygill knows who is in charge around here."

"Yes, yes, but first..." Marlene paused to get everyone's attention. "First, however, we must know exactly what goes on in that school."

"Ask the children!"

"Make the kids tell us."

"Ask them? I've tried. I've asked Karen a dozen times; she won't say anything," Mrs. Whiting said. "The most I've ever got her to admit is, 'It's a secret.' Now what kind of answer is that?"

"I can't get a thing out of Michael either," Cecile Hege said. "He's usually so talkative I have to tell him to shut up. I don't know what's happened, but this year when it comes to talking about school—"

"Marvin will tell me! I'll see to that!" Marlene's voice turned hard. "One way or another I'll get it out of him. I don't know why he wants to protect that teacher anyway. After all, she's the one who hurt him and took away his prize. He'll tell me or else!"

"Calm down, dear," her husband said soothingly. He picked up two strips of paper on which he had jotted down notes. "I believe we must do several things if we want changes to take place. First, of course, is to find out what's going on from the children. But remember, a child's word carries little weight against a teacher unless we can make several of them tell us the truth."

"Why don't we call in Miss Perkins?" Gerald Jenkins's father said. "After all, she was principal last year. She ought to be glad to get her job back and to set that school in order. And if she knows we'll back her all the way, I think she'd tell us."

*

From his upstairs bedroom, Marvin heard almost everything said. At first he hadn't tried to listen, but the loud voices easily carried that far. He thought about the first prize. He hadn't minded so much. He cared only because his mother had been upset about it. Since the announcement of the winners, at least once a day she brought up the topic. "You were cheated out of what was rightfully yours," was her most common statement.

He tried to tell her once that he hadn't tried very hard. And it was just an old prize anyway. He had gotten so interested in learning Spanish and in his geometry book, he had neglected his paper. Three times Mrs. Bennett had reminded him that he had to work hard.

But one thing, Marvin decided, he would never, never betray Mrs. Bennett. Not for anything. He had promised.

"I love you, Mrs. Bennett," he said to the darkness.

22

THE NEXT EVENING, EDWINA PERKINS DROVE TO THE BAGNULL HOME. As she waited for the door to open, she wondered if she ought to have come after all. The message, brought to her that morning by Marvin in a note, had both confused and depressed her.

Twice she had started to talk to Ophelia about the note—even to ask her advice. But then, she reminded herself, it might not be a serious problem. "And they are my students—and I am doing most of the upper-grades teaching now," she said aloud. "Perhaps they want to talk about their children's progress."

But inwardly, Edwina knew it was serious. As she walked from her Packard to the house, she admitted that she had lied to herself because she hadn't wanted to tell Mrs. Bennett.

The message had read simply:

> My dear Miss Perkins, would you be willing to meet this evening at seven with a few concerned parents? We are with you and wish to see our school straightened out.
>
> Marlene Bagnull

"Come in, come in!" Marlene almost shouted as she pulled the younger woman inside and embraced her briefly before she helped her take off her coat.

Edwina Perkins glanced around the room and saw Mr. Bagnull, the Whitings, and the Leeches. Five other parents arrived right behind her.

Miss Perkins nodded to each of them, then waited until Mr. Bagnull offered her a chair. "Please. Please, sit down, Miss Perkins. Marlene will bring you a cup of coffee."

"Thank you," she said. She did not really want coffee; yet she felt unwilling to refuse. Sitting stiffly in the chair, she gazed around the room and tried not to show her nervousness. She twisted her hands.

"You weren't told much about why we wanted you to come tonight," Mr. Bagnull said. "But we've decided to talk frankly with you and—uh, may I call you Edwina?" A stiff nod from the teacher and he continued, "We've heard a number of distressing reports about North Prairie School this year. Ever since Mrs. Bennett came, you understand. It appears she has buffaloed her way in, taken over, and relegated you to nothing but some kind of assistant."

"And we also know," Marlene said, as she stood in front of Edwina with a tray, "that you've been too sweet to argue with her. And, I imagine, too concerned for the students to make any serious complaints. We've heard about it, all about it."

"You've heard! But who? I mean, who said anything? Why—"

"All the parents are in an uproar," Beth Watkins said. "And we've decided to get things settled before they get any worse."

"Miss Perk—uh, Edwina, we're sorry that Mrs. Bennett has come in and treated you so badly. We also realize that, in spite of her, uh, strange behavior, you've done a magnificent job with the children," Cecile Hege said.

"We like you. You're one of us," Marvin's father said. "You went to school out of state, but you grew up in this part of Illinois. You know us. You understand how we feel, Edwina, and we believe we can trust you." He leaned forward confidentially. "We have great plans for your future."

"What we mean," Mr. Jenkins interrupted, "is that we want you to become principal again after this year!" He slapped his pudgy hand on the rocker arm. "And we're going to see that you receive a large salary increment. All we want is your cooperation."

Miss Perkins looked puzzled. "Cooperation?"

Marlene, who now sat next to Edwina, embraced her. "You dear, dear person, Edwina. You must have suffered immensely. And yet, here you sit so calmly." She released the teacher but clutched her hands. "You are so loyal, even though Mrs. Bennett is clearly in the wrong."

"We've already demanded that you receive a salary increment of $100 and whatever additional money comes from being principal. And you know, Edwina, once you're a principal in good standing, even of a small school like ours, it becomes the stepping stone for bigger positions," Mr. Osborn said.

"You'll have our backing all the way," Mr. Bagnull added.

"What—what do you want me to do?" the teacher asked, voice quivering.

"Do? Only tell the truth. Be willing to talk to Mr. Pettygill with us and denounce Mrs. Bennett."

"Mrs. Bennett? Why? She's doing a fine job," she protested meekly. "The children love her and they learned so much and...and I think she's the best teacher in the world."

Marlene now took her hand and patted it. "You don't have to cover up for her. Certainly not with us, my dear."

"We appreciate your loyalty," Beth said. "But we've heard about how she cowered you the first day you returned to school. You came back in your weakened physical condition and—"

"Why, I don't think—"

"Didn't Mrs. Bennett take over your classes? Even after you returned? And you didn't ask for her help, did you? We understand that she made all the lesson plans, for her classes and for yours. Is that not correct?" Mr. Bagnull asked, beginning to sound like the lawyer he was.

"How did you know that?"

"We forced the children to tell us. So you no longer need to protect her. The things I've said—are they not correct?"

"Well, yes, but—"

"And did she tell you what to teach and how to teach?"

Too shocked to speak, Miss Perkins nodded.

"Did she make you merely her assistant, taking all the responsibility for lessons, teaching, planning, and even room arrangement?"

"In a way, I suppose you could say—"

"Is it true that Mrs. Bennett not only allows games—not merely an occasional game—but that most of the activities revolve around playing? And isn't it true that North Prairie does not currently follow the prescribed Lake County curriculum?"

"Well, yes, I mean, no, she doesn't follow the curriculum, but you see—"

"Don't defend her, my dear," Marlene said. "We're on your side. We want you to have the recognition you deserve." She patted the teacher's hand once again.

"It really wasn't like that. I mean, isn't like that. I mean—"

"We're not asking you to confront Mrs. Bennett in a courtroom," Mr. Bagnull said. "We're asking you only to confirm what we already know."

"Then we'll present it to Mr. Pettygill," Marlene said. "That's probably as far as it will have to go. Now, do you understand?"

"I think so," she mumbled. She dropped her head because she did not want to look at any of them.

"I admire your sense of loyalty to Mrs. Bennett," Marlene said, "but we have more important things to settle right now. And, Edwina, you're doing the right thing. Mrs. Bennett will never have to know what you've told us. It will be our secret."

Edwina Perkins still stared at the floor.

23

THE NEXT MORNING, EDWINA PERKINS ARRIVED AT SCHOOL twenty minutes early. She wanted to tell Ophelia everything before the classes started. But she never had the chance. As soon as she walked in, Ophelia called her over excitedly.

"Edwina! Edwina! I am so glad you have arrived early. For the past three days, I have been extremely concerned because the children have not satisfactorily understood the verb tenses, especially when to use the past participle. These children are bright enough so I think we can even make the second graders understand without using words like *participle.* Look, let me show you what I worked out last night."

Miss Perkins knew that when Mrs. Bennett had a problem on her mind, she often went without sleep until she figured out what to do.

Mrs. Bennett led the younger teacher to her desk where she had laid out a game, somewhat like Bingo, where children could visually recognize verb tenses. She had made a set for every child in the school.

"You must have been up all night doing this," Miss Perkins said, her resolve now gone and trying to keep the conversation on safe topics.

"Not quite," Ophelia replied. "I woke up about two o'clock this morning and I could not return to sleep. I suppose it had been bothering me all day yesterday. You tried so hard to teach them verb tense. There was nothing wrong with your instructions, but somehow they did not seem to grasp the concept. I knew we could discover an easier way."

After Mrs. Bennett explained the game, Miss Perkins said, "I believe this will work."

"And I think it would be a good idea if you taught this to the upper grades just before lunch while I work with the first graders on their sight words. They have done extremely well with sounds, but they are still weak in using sight-memory."

"Oh, but you could do so much better with the older children. I mean, it's your idea—"

"Nonsense. Does it matter who thought of the method? You can do it, you know."

"Yes, I suppose I can."

"You are an absolutely outstanding teacher. I'm delighted and amazed at the skills you've developed. I am fortunate to work alongside you."

Miss Perkins flushed with pleasure. "Thank you." Then the memory of the night before burst into her head. "I don't think I ought—I mean, I need to say—"

"Nonsense, Edwina. You can do it easily. And you know, you really are better with those older students than I am. No, you can do it. Agreed?"

"Yes, of course. And—and thank you." She took the material to the far side of the room and went over the game carefully. Not once did she look at Mrs. Bennett again before school started. If she had, Edwina Perkins knew she would have started to cry.

*

Miss Perkins didn't talk to Ophelia about the parents that day. Or the next. Or the rest of the week. And as each day passed, it became easier for her not to think about what she had done. She began hoping that nothing would come of that meeting with the parents. Maybe Mr. Pettygill had refused to listen.

Almost before she knew it, April had come and it was the end of the month. The warm breeze gently stroked her face as she walked across the school yard at recess time. The two apple trees behind the school had their first buds sneaking into the open. As she stared at the large maple tree in the corner of the playground, she saw two robins making a nest.

Miss Perkins became so absorbed in their activity she didn't hear the approaching car until it was almost at the school gates. She immediately recognized Reginald Forder's Chevrolet. As casually as she could, Edwina walked toward the school building and tried not to look in that direction. She was unsuccessful in her determination.

After Reginald parked his two-year-old Chevrolet, he hurried from the car and ran over to greet Miss Perkins. With his back to the students, he grabbed her hand and held it as long as he felt he could. "Miss Perkins, how good to see you again!" he said loudly.

"Yes, good to see you, Mr. Forder." The handshake lasted a long time, but none of the children seemed to notice.

"What brings you to our school, Mr. Forder?" she asked, keeping her voice as loud as his.

"Good news to share with you and Mrs. Bennett," he said and smiled. "Wait until we go inside." Then he whispered, "You—you're wonderful. I think about you every day. All the time."

She blushed. "I think about you all the time too."

*

Three minutes later, inside the room and with Mrs. Bennett's approval, Reginald Forder stood in front of the room. "I have carefully scored the achievement tests from this school as well as those for all unincorporated areas. I had them all checked by mid-March but, frankly, the results were...well, unusual. I have rechecked them. Then, to be absolutely sure, I asked three teachers from the Waukegan city schools to go through them. They are so unusual I suspected that dishonesty might be involved." He blushed slightly and turned toward Mrs. Bennett. "Not that I felt you would cheat, Mrs. Bennett, or—or you, Miss Perkins, but we have to be sure. We have had such cases before."

"And?" Mrs. Bennett asked.

"We carefully rechecked the papers. We even spent time on the computation figures on the worksheets that we insist you pass in with your examination." He looked at the students. "All this is to say, we're convinced that the tests are valid."

"What's 'valid' mean?" The first grader raised his hand at the same time.

"That means reliable, uh, honest," Reginald replied and smiled at the boy. "I'm glad you asked."

Reginald glanced at Edwina Perkins, then at Ophelia, and back to Edwina. "Remarkably, the results show that every student in North Prairie School—every single student, without exception—has scored a minimum of two years' achievement level above your actual grade. Most of you scored three or four years higher. We've never had this happen before. I checked the records, so I know. Not in any school."

Mrs. Bennett stood. "Class, this means that you've all done well in the tests you took before Christmas. For example, Catherine is in third grade. It means that, according to the test, she could be expected to do the work required of a student in fifth grade. Am I correct, Mr. Forder?"

"Yes, you are, Mrs. Bennett. Absolutely correct!"

"Even me?" Yvonne asked. "I'm above my grade level?"

"Even you. In fact, especially you. Uh, you are Yvonne Ortega? You've made a jump—" He shuffled through several sheets of paper. "You've gone from a third-grade level that was recorded last year. It was 3.0, which means the work expected of a student just entering the third grade. Your test scores have an overall average of 11.7. In other words, this is the work we could reasonably expect from someone in the seventh month of school in the eleventh grade."

"Muy bien," Marvin whispered.

"And, Miss Perkins, this is certainly your doing! You deserve as much credit as the students. The upper grades showed the most remarkable rise I've ever seen in test scores. I commend you for your exemplary work. I know you have put in many hours of planning and teaching and—"

"But I—I—" stammered Edwina.

"Yes, Miss Perkins has worked very hard," Mrs. Bennett said. "I have noticed her remarkable progress as a teacher since she started the year. Mr. Forder, she's extremely talented. She deserves every word of encouragement and appreciation."

"And of course, you do, too, Mrs. Bennett. You've obviously done a good job," Reginald said, but he stared at Edwina.

The children glanced at each other and shrugged. Ginger and Karen whispered to each other. Nickolas started to get out of his seat, but Max reached across the aisle and pushed him back. "If she wants you to speak up, she'll tell you."

"As a matter of fact," Reginald Forder said, reluctantly taking his eyes off Edwina and looking at the class once more, "I've come here because something has happened that I've never seen before. Miss Perkins, one of your students made a perfect score in the science area. So far as I know, and as our records show, this has only occurred in Illinois once. That was in 1934 before the achievement tests were as sophisticated and reliable. I have already made arrangements, providing his parents agree, to send him to Springfield next month. He will participate in a statewide competition for scholarships. He will be the only student not already in high school to compete. That's never happened before. Quite a remarkable achievement."

"Who is it?" Karen asked.

"The student is—Nickolas Harrison."

Clapping resounded through the school. Nickolas flushed both from pleasure and embarrassment. His penchant for a comeback deserted him and he smiled self-consciously. Ophelia Bennett stood beside him and laid her arm on his shoulder. "I have faith in you. We all know how hard you've worked. When you go to Springfield to compete on the state level, you will do even better. I know you will."

24

TEN MINUTES BEFORE LUNCH PERIOD, and long after Reginald Forder had gone, a delegation of parents came en masse to the school door. Mr. Bagnull walked inside and said, "Mrs. Bennett, we have come here on rather urgent business. We'd like to see both you and Miss Perkins alone."

Ophelia directed the children to get their lunches and go outside to the playground. "Nickolas will be in charge," she added.

Yvonne ran into the girls' lavatory as the rest of the class picked up lunch bags and boxes and headed toward the playground.

After the children were outside, Ralph Whiting locked the door from the inside. "So we'll not have kids bustin' in here to interrupt us."

"Mrs. Bennett, I'll explain to you exactly why we have come," Mr. Bagnull said. "We are six parents, representing the parents of North Prairie School—"

"Representing all the parents?" Mrs. Bennett asked calmly.

"No, of course not all, but certainly most of them. Enough that we have gone to Mr. Pettygill and discussed this matter with him."

"I see," Mrs. Bennett said as she sat down at her desk. She offered them seats, but they all refused.

"Our business won't take long, Mrs. Bennett. We are here to say, first of all, we disapprove of the way you have run North Prairie School. Games, playing—these are not the ways we learn, Mrs. Bennett. Just last week I asked Marvin if he had memorized the multiplication tables and he said that you didn't teach that way."

"And another thing," interrupted Mr. Whiting as he stepped up next to Mr. Bagnull, "you are not responsible for the older children. That's Miss Perkins's position. You came in here and just took over—like some dictator. We've had enough of that kind of behavior."

"Perhaps there is no need to get upset with a lot of words," Marlene Bagnull said as she handed Ophelia Bennett a typewritten sheet of paper. "Here are twelve charges against you made by parents and we're ready to file them with Mr. Pettygill's office. Of course, we don't have to file them—" She revealed her small, gleaming teeth.

"What are you asking of me?"

"First, your resignation effective at the end of the school year. If we do not file charges, there will be nothing against your record," Marlene continued in a matter-of-fact voice that was betrayed by the hardness in her eyes.

"And—"

"And," she turned to face Miss Perkins, "Miss Perkins will become acting principal until the end of the year. Next year she will be appointed as the principal. She will assume complete authority over upper-grade children. She may move them back into the other classroom if she chooses."

"How does Miss Perkins feel about this?" Ophelia Bennett asked, her eyes focused on the shorter woman.

"I—I didn't ask for it, honest I didn't," she said meekly. "Please, Mrs. Bennett, I didn't mean to—"

"I accept your terms with this stipulation: You may not tell the children anything. I would not want them upset. I shall retain the title of principal, but I shall defer to Miss Perkins in all matters and ask her advice when needed. Furthermore, I shall make application for a new position next year. Is that satisfactory with you?"

"Yes, yes, of course," the parents echoed each other. Mr. Bagnull smiled. Mr. Whiting showed obvious relief. Mrs. Bagnull said, "I'm glad you weren't difficult about this."

"But what about the results of the achievement tests?" burst out Yvonne as she ran from the girls' room. "Don't you know that our school has scored the highest in the county and that it is all because of Mrs. Bennett? She did for us what no one has done. I could not even speak English properly when she came, and she's the best teacher in the world." The girl broke down with sobs.

Ophelia Bennett cradled the sobbing girl. She slowly stroked the plaited black hair and patted her thin shoulders. "It is all right, Yvonne," she repeated several times.

"We don't care about achievement tests! We care about morale! About teaching properly!" Mr. Whiting shouted.

"We've heard about Yvonne, too!" Mr. Jenkins said. "You've made her your special pet. And you've neglected other students."

"You tried to force our children to learn Spanish. We're not having any more of that kind of thing!" Marlene added, "Including my son."

Ophelia stared for several seconds at the parents, her face impassive. "I have given this child only what she deserves—an equal chance, the right to learn. I have done no more for her than I would for any of the other thirty-two pupils." She kept her tone calm, but narrowed her eyes.

Yvonne clung more tightly to her teacher.

"Thank you, Mrs. Bennett," Marlene said. "Let's go now." The parents turned and headed toward the door. Mr. Kent opened it for the others to precede him.

Edwina Perkins rushed over to Ophelia, started to grab her, and then dropped her arms. "I'm sorry, Ophelia. I'm so sorry. Please. I didn't mean—"

Ophelia Bennett loosened Yvonne's grip and whispered, "Excuse me, please." She got out of her seat and walked rigidly toward the girls' lavatory.

Yvonne started to to run after her.

But Ophelia murmured, "Please, I—I need to be alone. For a few minutes."

*

Yvonne walked slowly back to her own desk, laid her head down, and sobbed.

Miss Perkins did not move. "What have I done?" she asked half-aloud. "What have I done?"

The shock of the outside door banging open and against the wall brought Miss Perkins to awareness of the room. She scrambled to her feet and moved toward the children. They came in as a group. She could tell from the angered faces and clenched fists that they knew.

"I ought to break you into pieces with my bare hands!" Nickolas said.

"You gave away our secret!" Ginger accused.

"You're terrible, Miss Perkins," freckle-faced Michael yelled. "I hate you!"

"No, please, I—I—"

"We heard everything from outside the boys' lavatory window," Nickolas said. "I boosted Marvin up and he opened it. You just wanted Mrs. Bennett's job and you were jealous because she's such a good teacher!"

"No, no, that's not true!"

"And we were just getting to like you," Max said. "But you don't need to worry. None of us—not one of us—likes you now."

"I thought you were my friend!" Larry bellowed.

"They're going to chase Mrs. Bennett away," Yvonne said through her sobs. "I won't go to school anymore, if she doesn't teach!"

"It's your fault, Miss Perkins. And I hate you," Catherine yelled.

"And I heard everything you said to them when you were at my house that night! You squealer! You ruined everything!" Marvin said.

"I—I know I've failed and I'm—" She took out her handkerchief and started to cry.

"Your dumb old tears won't make any difference," Nickolas said. "We don't want you in our school anymore."

"My, I didn't realize the lunch period had passed so quickly," Mrs. Bennett said brightly as she walked back into the room. She glanced at her watch. "Hmmm, actually, you are ten minutes early. Someone must have gotten confused about the time. But never mind. As long as you are all back inside, we have a Spanish folk dance Yvonne wants to teach us. First we all have to get into a circle—"

"Mrs. Bennett, please. This is not a time for games," Karen said, hunching up one shoulder as she had seen Claudette Colbert do in the film, *Midnight.*

Ophelia nodded slowly as her eyes swept across the room. Edwina kept her head buried in the handkerchief. "All right. Everyone sit down. First we shall talk, and then we shall learn the folk dance."

The children ambled to their desks.

Edwina heard one low whisper, "You'll find out just how mean we can be if you try to teach next year." She spun around but could not detect who had spoken.

"It saddens me that all of this has happened. I am also extremely sorry that you children heard what went on. I had hoped to spare you that much."

"But you're not coming back, are you? Next year, I mean?" Boy asked.

"That is true. I will not return to North Prairie."

"You have to. We need you!"

"You can go to that old Mr. Pettygill yourself, Mrs. Bennett."

"We'll all go. We'll tell him the truth!"

Ophelia raised her hands. "You are all speaking at once. I know you are angry and hurt and probably quite confused by all of this. I am going to remain here at North Prairie for another six weeks. School will continue as before. Then we shall talk about my leaving. If you have enjoyed school so far, then make these last weeks happy for me. Please do this for me."

"But how can we, when we know you're going away?" Michael asked.

"We may never see you again. Not ever," Karen said, imitating Vivien Leigh in *Gone with the Wind.* "And whatever shall we do?"

"I am still here. I am not leaving yet."

"Mrs. Bennett, what can we do if you leave? If Miss Perkins comes back or some other stupid teacher, we'll have to go back to all that dumb stuff again," Boy said.

"And she'll boss us around," Catherine said.

"And shout at us the way she did last year!" Yvonne added.

"We'll continue the rest of the year the way we've been doing it," Edwina said limply. "I'll take care of reports and records that have to go to the county. But as far as the classroom itself, we'll go on as before."

The students relaxed somewhat, but they sat in silence.

"And I'm sorry you hate me. I've tried to be a good teacher." She lowered her head and sobbed. "Several of your parents intimidated—frightened me. But I let them do it. I've tried so hard to be a good teacher and I—I guess I was just jealous of Mrs. Bennett. That's why they were able to make me betray her. She's such a wonderful teacher and you kept telling her how good she is. And I resented it because I wanted to be a good teacher." She burst into tears again.

"I don't hate you, Miss Perkins," Yvonne said softly. "I did before, because you thought I was stupid. I thought I was stupid, too. But it's been different this year, especially since Christmas. I just don't want Mrs. Bennett to leave."

"She helped me and you got all the credit," Nickolas said. "But I guess I kinda understand."

"Thank you. Thank you for being more kind to me than I've been to you."

"Children, you have learned a valuable lesson today. It is called forgiveness. People often do foolish things. Miss Perkins did not wish or intend to hurt me. I know that. And perhaps we have failed Miss Perkins. She has worked hard, very hard. She has done much for you, and I could not have accomplished it by myself. Miss Perkins is a gifted teacher and she will do an outstanding job."

"Yeah, this year maybe she did, but last year—" Nickolas said.

"She used to scream at you, but that was not because she hated you. She was afraid—afraid of failing, afraid of doing a poor job. But she loves you; she truly loves you."

"Mrs. Bennett, we understand, but that's not what really upsets us," Max said. "Most of all, we're upset because *you're* leaving us."

"Yes, I know. And I love each of you. But you can love me and still love Miss Perkins. God gives all of us the ability to love more than one person. You do not have to settle for just one friend. Or only one teacher."

"I don't hate you, do I?" Michael asked before he planted a wet kiss on Edwina Perkins's arm.

"Okay, I'm sorry, Miss Perkins," Nickolas said. "I really like you and you've been good to us this year. It's really been fun."

Others followed Nickolas.

Ophelia waited until everyone had had a chance to speak to Edwina.

"Good, now for our Spanish folk dance. Let's push all the desks against the wall."

*

After the students had gone, Mrs. Bennett made last-minute changes in her lesson plans for the next day. She went to the west side of the room to close all the windows before leaving. Miss Perkins had been engrossed in her work at the back of the room. She looked up and their eyes met.

"Good night, my dear." Ophelia returned to her desk to pick up her purse.

"Don't leave yet. Please. Let me talk to you."

"Of course." She walked back to Edwina's desk and pulled up a chair. She sat down.

"How can you be so kind to me? I have hurt you...betrayed you."

"I was hurt and I will not deny that. Deeply hurt. I went to the girls' lavatory and had a good cry. But I do not blame you."

"Don't blame me? They wrote down those twelve charges because of what they pumped out of me. They really didn't know much of anything. Just a word or two from the children. The children knew how to keep quiet. I was the one who—"

"You were not wicked, only weak. Perhaps a bit foolish, but not wicked. There is a difference. And because I know you did it out of weakness, it is easy to put that behind us. If you had plotted against me, I would have had a much more difficult time forgiving you."

"But how—how can you be so forgiving?"

Mrs. Bennett leaned back in her chair and stared into space. After a lengthy silence, she said, "I can forgive you because I've been forgiven. A long time ago I met God in a personal way. I understood what Jesus tried to say to us when He died on the cross. He prayed for God to forgive those who crucified Him. I did not crucify Jesus, but I have hurt people, dishonored God."

"You? You're the best person I've ever met! Why, why you're perfect, in every way."

"Thank you, but I am not the perfect person. That fits only Jesus. And if He could forgive, so can I."

"I don't understand."

"Perhaps you will one day."

"Oh, I hope so. And I hope I can learn to forgive as easily as you do."

"You can. Yes, you can when you know God as your personal friend—as your best friend. And you will. Yes, my dear, you will. I know that. God has promised me."

"Promised? I don't understand."

Mrs. Bennett embraced the younger woman, but she did not answer.

25

WARM MAY BREEZES FILLED NORTH PRAIRIE SCHOOL. The scent of two lilac bushes permeated the building. A bee occasionally flew into the classroom, buzzed around, and flew back out again. Jonquils and tulips appeared each morning on the teachers' desks, usually brought by Ginger.

Lessons continued as they had since the beginning of the year. The one topic of conversation no one discussed was the future of Ophelia Bennett.

A few children bragged of upcoming vacation trips. Catherine's family always drove to Michigan for the summer months; others hinted of summer camp. Miss Perkins had mentioned her plans to spend the summer in graduate school.

On the last day of school, in early June, the children returned to straighten up the classroom and conclude with a party. Each child carried two boxes—a gift for each teacher. They marked the gifts and laid them out, those for Miss Perkins on one end of the table and those for Mrs. Bennett on the other.

At 11:00, Mrs. Whiting, Mrs. Murphy, and Mrs. Bagnull brought cookies, lemonade, and a cake, and left immediately afterward. After the teachers had opened their presents, thanked everyone, and had completed the cleaning-up, Mrs. Bennett asked everyone to sit down.

"I want to say good-bye to you, but I find it extremely difficult to do. This is my eighteenth year of teaching and you are, without any doubt, the brightest, most eager students I have ever taught. I shall enjoy the classes where I teach after this, but none of them can ever be quite as meaningful as this one. You—all of you—will hold a special place in my heart and in my memory."

She wiped tears from her eyes and began to walk around the classroom. Going to each student, one at a time, she spoke words of appreciation and encouragement. She patted one on the cheek, another on the shoulder.

After she had gone completely around the room, she stopped in front of Edwina Perkins. "You are a fine teacher. You must put behind you the circumstances that have brought you to your new position. This is where you belong. This is where you will grow."

"I'm so sorry and so ashamed of—"

She took both of the young woman's hands in hers. "I have forgiven you. Now you must learn to forgive yourself."

Ophelia Bennett circled the room again. She wore that deep, thoughtful expression that the children had long recognized as deep concentration. She stopped pacing and said, "And one thing more before our party. I want to make you a promise, a special promise. Please listen carefully to the words, and do not be concerned if you do not understand it now."

"What kind of promise?" one of the girls asked.

"I shall start with this." Ophelia took a small notebook out of her dress pocket. "At the beginning of the year, I wrote each of your names here." She held up the book. "Every morning before I left my house, I prayed for each of you by name. I asked God to strengthen you in the weak areas of your life, and enable you to behave kindly in the strong ones."

Michael Hege shook his head. "I don't—"

She held up her hand to silence him. "This I shall explain. In areas where we are strong, we tend to look down on those who are not as able or as gifted. I have prayed, for example, that Max would understand his musical ability as a gift—a gift not only for him, but to use it to enrich others' lives."

Michael smiled. "I understand that."

"At the beginning of the year, most of you thought Yvonne was stupid. I can tell you now that she is not only extremely intelligent but a gifted teacher. I often pray that she will use that teaching ability throughout the rest of her life."

"Oh, I will. I know that I am going to be a teacher," Yvonne said. "You have shown me how you can change other people. Look at what you have done for me."

"I know I'm different too." Nickolas laughed before he said, "You started to work on me that first day when I marked on my desk."

Several others expressed appreciation and told of important moments in their lives that school year.

Ophelia calmly waited for the class to quiet before she raised her palm. "Now there is one more thing I wish to say to you. I have a gift for you. I give it to you in the form of a promise."

"A promise?" Michael said. "You mean that you'll stay here?"

She shook her head. "I promise that as long as I am alive, I will pray for each of you by name every day. I shall ask God to show me what you need—which is the manner I have used in praying for you from the beginning."

"Will God really show you what we need?" Max asked. "What I need?"

"Yes, God has so far and I believe God will continue to do so."

"And you've prayed for *me*?" Nickolas asked and then blushed. "Every day? Even when I—"

"Yes, Nickolas. For each of you. I have prayed for you when you had problems in English grammar or spelling. But besides that, there are two things I have asked God for each day."

"Two things?" Karen asked.

"First, that each of you would become the best possible person God could make you into. It would break my heart if any of you settled for anything less than using all your potential and living in ways to help other people. Second, I pray that each of you will have a personal relationship with God—that He will become your closest friend."

"I go to church on Sunday," Karen said. "I *have* to go."

"So do I." Ginger sighed.

"That is not what I meant. Going to church is fine, but in itself that is not enough. I want you to know God as your friend—someone you can talk to every day, and you know He hears you—not just when you go to a church."

"Oh," one of the girls answered.

"Perhaps that does not sound like much of a promise to you," Ophelia Bennett said. But I sincerely hope that it will become meaningful in the years to come." She paced the room slowly, then settled against the edge of her desk. "I want to tell you something else, something very important. It may bore you, but please listen."

"You couldn't bore us." Max grinned. "Not ever."

Her eyes sparkled in acknowledgment. Then she told them about her coming to North Prairie. "Mr. Pettygill gave me two days to make a decision. The next two days became extremely important to me."

*

After she left Mr. Pettygill's office, she had driven to Shiloh Park in Zion. No one else was around, which was exactly what she wanted. She sat in a swing, hardly aware that she was pushing herself lightly.

I do not know what to do. God, please help me. Is it not time for me to teach where it is easy? Where I can teach and serve You that way? Is it not time for me to let others wage the battles?

She continued to pray, hardly moving for more than an hour. Around her the trees had already begun to change. The oaks, maples, and poplars presented a patina of color. High clouds tracked across the azure sky. Squirrels leaped from tree to tree, but she barely noticed them.

She continued to pray.

No answer came. She prayed still more.

She stayed until subdued hues painted the western sky. A warm breeze fluttered, carrying with it the distinctive fragrance of honeysuckle. Sighing, she got out of the swing and walked to her car. She felt no closer to an answer than when she had come hours earlier.

When she walked into the house, Richard was sitting at the table, listening to the radio. She had no idea how much of it he understood. She hugged him and then prepared scrambled eggs and fried potatoes for his evening meal. She ate nothing, but she did drink two cups of tea.

Once Richard was comfortably in bed, she went into their spare bedroom and knelt. For almost an hour, she poured out her concerns to God. Still, she felt no relief from the burden.

She got up, paced the room, and then knelt again and prayed. Three times this happened. Finally, weary and despairing, she went to bed, but sleep refused to come.

Finally, just before the dawn, she said, "All right, God, I surrender. Whatever You want. I will not fight You."

At that moment, she received her answer.

26

AFTER OPHELIA BENNETT TOLD THEM, her eyes filled with tears. She wiped them with her lace handkerchief.

"Oh, don't cry, please don't cry," Karen begged, perfectly imitating Norma Shearer from the film *The Women.*

"I am not sad," she said and wiped her eyes. "This is difficult for me to speak about, but this is the truth. I heard God speak—not in actual words, not out loud as I am speaking right now—but with a message so powerful that I have never doubted what I heard."

"Swell! What'd God say?" Nickolas asked.

"God reminded me of a story—of Jesus' final meeting with His disciples, His followers—before He was crucified."

"Yes, I know that story. It took place in the upper room," Max said. "We studied that in Sunday school."

"Who knows the promise Jesus gave those followers?"

No one raised a hand.

"Jesus promised that He would be with them. He was going to die and He knew that, but He promised to send the Holy Spirit to them. He said the Holy Spirit would teach them and help them understand and be with them all throughout their lives, no matter what happened."

"Yes, I do remember that," Boy said. "I read it last night." Embarrassment colored his face. "I, uh, I've been reading the Bible a lot since you came here."

"And what was the promise?" she asked.

"That He would send them a—He called it a comfort or something like that."

"A *comforter.* That is correct." She closed her eyes for several seconds before she looked at the children again. "This may sound a trifle strange, but this is exactly what happened as I lay on my bed. God assured me that each of you would respond to me because I would be here as an instrument of God's love to each of you."

"You have already been to me," Yvonne said.

"Me too," Max added.

Others echoed their words.

"There was more. God made me understand that there would be many difficult times, that some of you would fight me and that—I am so sorry to say this aloud but it is important—that even my co-teacher, a person I would love and trust, would betray me."

Edwina Perkins burst into tears. "I'm so—"

"Forgive me for this, my dear. It was not to hurt you, but to explain that God prepared me. I knew what you would do...that you would fail that test." She laid her hands on Edwina's shoulders. "God also assured me that after this, you would not fail. I knew, even before we ever met, that your betrayal in a moment of weakness would become your strength and that God would use you to teach many, many children."

"And we did respond, didn't we?" Boy asked.

"Yes, that is correct. Now I must leave you, and here is the promise. I shall take this notebook with me. Every day that God allows me to live in this world I *will* pray for you." She bit her lower lip in concentration. Finally she said, "That is not precisely what I wish to say. The promise is more than my praying for you."

Everyone stared at her and waited for her to speak again.

"God sent me to North Prairie. I knew before coming that it would end like this, that I would be rejected." She held up her hand. "Not by you, of course. God enabled me to know it was coming, but before it came, my purpose, my task, was to express love and concern for each one of you—love that came from God. To the best of my ability, I have done that."

"You surely did," Marvin said and others echoed his voice.

"After today, when you pray, you will still hear my voice. I am not God or any supernatural person, but my role was to bring God to you, and to enable you to see how much your heavenly Father loves you."

This time when she paused no one said anything.

"When you pray for help, many times—probably not every time, but often, and especially when you have the most difficult decisions to make—you will hear my voice. You will remember me and remember the things I have taught you. When you pray sincerely, somewhere deep inside your heads, you will hear my voice, just as if I were standing here before you."

Ophelia's gaze went from child to child. She felt she had not said it well.

"You mean, it's like, uh, like when Jesus went away," Boy said. "He couldn't come back to them, but they prayed and the Holy Spirit spoke to them and that kept them thinking about Jesus. Maybe," he shrugged, "maybe when they heard a voice, they heard the voice of Jesus speaking. Is that what you mean?"

"Yes, exactly. You are quite young, but you have insight. You understand spiritual things so readily."

"So you mean you're going to pray for us every day?" Max asked. "Even though you won't be here? And we won't see you? And when we pray, really pray, God will let us hear you. He'll answer us in a way that we can hear your voice. Is that what you mean?"

"Yes, and, you know, the Holy Spirit can speak to me as well. I am going to ask God to help me know whenever any of you needs special prayer or has a problem." She moved about the room, lightly touching the cheek or shoulder of each child. "Yes, I will pray for each one of you every day. You can rest assured that no matter how difficult life or problems become for you, God knows and will show me how to pray for you."

"I want you to pray for me," Max said. "I don't guess I really understand what you said, but if you think I need it, I want it, so will you really do that?"

"Yes."

"I feel the same way," Boy answered, followed by others.

"And please don't forget me," Edwina Perkins murmured.

"You have my promise—each of you. Oh, it has been a good year, has it not? You have learned so much. You children...oh, I have never been so proud of any group of students as I am of you."

"We still don't want you to leave," Michael said.

"Please, can't you stay?" another asked.

"Can't we talk to our parents or something?"

"I could talk to Mr. Pettygill," Edwina Perkins said, but Ophelia shook her head.

"Can we go where you're teaching next time?" The freckle-faced boy raised his hand as he asked.

Ophelia lifted her hand, waiting for silence again. "Please do not make it more difficult for me. I love you and I am assured that each of you knows that. We have had a splendid year together." She gazed intently from face to face. "I am leaving today. I may never see any of you again. I have done my best for you. Keep your minds and hearts open to God. Many wonderful things still lie ahead. I want you to be the finest people and most dedicated individuals you are capable of becoming. God will help you. I know that."

"Can we write to you?" Karen asked.

"Should have said *may*," the freckle-faced boy called out as he raised his hand.

Ophelia chuckled. "Yes, it should have been *may* instead of *can*, and yes, you may write to me. I shall leave my address with Miss Perkins. When you return Tuesday for report cards, you will have it."

Marvin grinned. Yvonne dropped her head and tears slid gently down her cheeks. Nickolas buttoned and unbuttoned the top button on his shirt.

"But—but won't we ever see you again?" Ginger asked.

"I do not know. Certainly you will never see me here again as your teacher. But you do not really need me anymore. I believe in every one of you. God has assured me that each of you will do well. You have so many good and remarkable things to present to the world. You will make this a better world. Each of you."

"You can't leave. Look how you've helped us," Max said. "We're all different because—"

"Yes, you are different. And perhaps that alone says this is the best time for me to leave. I have done my best. Now I expect you to continue learning. I also expect you to help the new children as they enter this school next year."

"We will! We will!" the children chorused.

Mrs. Bennett nodded to Edwina Perkins, who stood and announced, "Now we may have our party. Everything is ready."

At the end of the party, Mrs. Bennett said, "When you leave, let us not say good-bye. Instead, we shall join hands and sing a lovely song. It is called 'Blest Be the Tie That Binds.' It is a song about God's love that binds us to each other."

*

The students played games, ate their refreshments and drank the lemonade. Four upper-grade children volunteered to clean up. The others went home.

"I shall never forget any of you. Not ever!" Ophelia said as they filed past her.

"We'll never forget you either," Larry said.

*

The cleanup quickly completed, three of the volunteers left. Nickolas stayed and helped Mrs. Bennett carry out the last boxes of her material. Many items she declined and showed Nickolas where to leave them. "I think Miss Perkins will want this next year."

By one o'clock even Nickolas had no reason to linger. He nodded and saluted as he left.

Edwina Perkins kept herself busy at her own desk, working on report cards. After that, she stacked and re-stacked papers.

Finally she got up from her desk, walked over, and sat next to Mrs. Bennett. "You've taught me so much. I feel as though I've been one of your students rather than a peer."

Mrs. Bennett patted the younger woman on the cheek. "If that is the case, you have been the brightest." She handed her a slip of paper. "Here is my new address—at least that's the school address. Anytime you want to write...anytime...I should love to hear from you."

Miss Perkins impulsively hugged her. "You're the most wonderful person I've ever known."

"I am not wonderful, Edwina, but I love you. And I love these thirty-three children. Perhaps knowing another person loves us makes that person seem wonderful. Do you suppose that is the case?"

Before Miss Perkins could answer she became aware of a car racing toward North Prairie School. With opened windows the sound carried easily. Ophelia raised her head and watched the vehicle grow larger. Edwina stood and looked.

Ophelia recognized Reginald Forder's Chevrolet.

The car braked noisily and, seconds later, two scrambling pairs of feet thudded across the hardwood floor. Mr. Pettygill, puffing from the exertion, followed yards behind Reginald.

"Hello, Edwina." Reginald beamed. "Uh, hello, Mrs. Bennett."

"I was afraid I'd miss you. I am thankful you are still here," gasped Mr. Pettygill between breaths. He ignored Edwina Perkins and looked at Mrs. Bennett.

"I was just leaving."

"I won't waste a lot of your time, dear Mrs. Bennett," the silver-haired superintendent said. "I fear a grave injustice has been done to you. Several parents took it upon themselves to demand your resignation from North Prairie—quite without my sanction, of course. I've only heard about it this morning. I must protest: I want you to stay. In fact, I insist upon it. With your return as principal, I can assure you that your salary will be increased at least 150 dollars next year."

"Thank you, Mr. Pettygill, but I have already signed a contract."

"But you cannot—you cannot! We need you here. I shall transfer you to any school you choose in the system. Just stay," protested Mr. Pettygill, his skin now flushed red. He stopped and swiped his perspiring face with a handkerchief. "I deeply admire your work. You are an exemplary teacher, the best quality—"

"I told Mr. Pettygill about the outstanding work your students have done," interrupted Reginald. "You see, Miss Perkins explained it all to me last night. Uh, we worked late together. She said you'd done most of the work here at North Prairie and helped her look good. I know you took the blame when the parents rose up."

Edwina Perkins took Reginald's hand, but she faced Ophelia. "I didn't know what to do. You wouldn't let me go to Mr. Pettygill."

Reginald, aware Edwina had taken his hand, blushed. "I think you're swell, Mrs. Bennett, just absolutely swell." The brightness of Reginald's dark eyes glowed.

"You are wonderful," Edwina said.

"The essays the pupils wrote were submitted to state contests this year," Reginald said. "We should have had the results five weeks ago, but they got lost in the mail or something. Anyway, we found out only yesterday afternoon. Pupils from North Prairie have won three of the first six places in the state. So you know now why Mr. Pettygill suddenly realizes your value. He does not want you to leave. Neither do I."

"I've always appreciated you, Mrs. Bennett. Naturally, I was not aware of how truly excellent you really were until—"

"Mr. Pettygill called Mrs. Bagnull this morning," Reginald interrupted again, "and informed her of the achievement. Frankly, she was embarrassed, especially since Marvin placed second in the entire state. If she knew how to apologize, I'm sure she'd be here right now. That's why we came running out here."

"I can handle this, *Mister* Forder, if you do not mind!" Mr. Pettygill brushed Reginald aside. "The important thing is, we want you to stay on here. We are quite willing to renew your contract."

"Thank you, but it is too late, Mr. Pettygill. I have made other arrangements. You were informed of my intentions nearly two months ago. I have already signed a contract with a school in the central part of the state. And you know that no ethical teacher ever goes back on a signed contract."

Mrs. Bennett rose from her desk and kissed Edwina Perkins on the cheek. As she shook hands with Reginald, she leaned down and whispered in his ear, "You are greatly blessed to have such a fine woman in love with you."

"Yes'm," he replied, blushing again.

"Mr. Pettygill, good-bye."

"Please! My dear Mrs. Bennett—"

Ophelia Bennett picked up her purse and walked out of North Prairie School.

Epilogue

Chicago Illinois, 1981

"MICHAEL HEGE! WHY, YOU CAME AFTER ALL!" The dark-haired woman rushed forward and put one hand over her nametag.

He stared at the woman's unlined face, not sure who she was. He was almost ready to ask her name when recognition filled his eyes. "Karen! You're—you're not little Karen Whiting who had that really bad crush on Nickolas Harrison?"

"Yes! I'm Karen—Karen *Harrison!*"

"So you got him, after all?"

"Oh, well, he got me, too, you know." She hugged him.

"Do you know me?" a low-voiced woman behind him asked.

Michael released Karen and turned in surprise. "You—you're—"

"Yvonne Ortega."

"No! You're beautiful! I mean, I guess, I know how old you have to be, but I'd—I'd guess you weren't more than thirty-five."

When he kissed her cheek, her jasmine fragrance filled his nostrils. Her black hair and eyes that once had seemed so foreign now radiated a brightness that kept his eyes focused on her high cheekbones and soft skin.

"You are absolutely one of the most gorgeous women I've ever—"

"I ought to be easy to recognize," she said, cutting him off. "After all, I was the only minority student back then." She grabbed his hand. "Come on, let's go around and say hello to everyone. I've kept in touch with most of them over the years so I don't need reintroductions." She led him from the doorway to a small group near the hors d'oeuvres.

Five minutes later, the door opened and a squat-figured woman, white-haired and wearing no makeup, entered the room. As she took each pain-filled step, she leaned on a cane for support. She peered at the faces through her thick glasses and smiled widely as various people waved to her. Her gaze moved from face to face. "You all look so wonderful," she said as she limped forward. "So wonderful. You've all grown up."

"Miss Perkins! I'm so glad you came," Karen said. "It wouldn't have been a real reunion without you."

"Thank you. Only I'm not Miss Perkins anymore, you know."

"That's right, you're Mrs.—"

"Mrs. Reginald Forder," the owner of the name said as he walked in. Reginald had remained as thin as he had been forty years earlier. The heavy-lensed glasses obscured his dark eyes. "We couldn't let this go by without being here. Besides, Boy sent us a special invitation. He insisted that we come tonight." He looked around. "She isn't here yet?"

"Not yet, but she will be." Karen squinted at the tiny figures on her wristwatch. "Why, by my watch she's already three minutes late. Promptness was always a big thing with her and now she's late for her own party. We'll have to scold her for that!"

"She's not coming!"

Everyone stared at the tall, thin man who stood in one corner.

"She's not coming!" he said even louder.

"How do you know she's not coming?" Nickolas Harrison asked.

"I'm Boy Masters, everyone," he said. "Mrs. Bennett isn't coming."

"Of course she is," Karen said. "That's a terrible thing to—"

"She's not com—" Boy choked and tears seeped down his face. "She's not coming because—because she died last week."

"Died? Oh, no—" A shocked Karen looked as if she might faint. Nickolas wrapped his arm around her.

"That's a cruel joke," Yvonne said.

"No joke, Yvonne. It's true." He wiped the tears from his eyes and took several deep breaths. "If you'll all sit down for a minute, I'll explain. I'm only doing what Mrs. Bennett asked me to do tonight."

"Asked you?" Yvonne echoed.

Boy held up his hand and waited until they had pulled up chairs and sat down. In their attempts to accept Boy's words, no one looked at anyone else. Two of the women cried softly. Nickolas held his wife tightly.

Yvonne clasped Michael's hand. "Ohh, it can't be."

"I've kept in contact with Ophelia Bennett. Many of you did, too. I never had much of a home life and she, well, she became like a mother to me. She wrote me every week. Even paid for part of my college education, although I didn't know it until years later. The school officials told me I had won a scholarship."

Boy pulled out his handkerchief and blew his nose. "I've been an ordained clergyman—a Methodist pastor—since 1954. Ophelia Bennett had that kind of an effect on my life. Each morning I knew she prayed for me, and I knew that no matter how bad things were, I could face the day." He took a series of long, slow breaths. His eyes moistened again and he wiped them with his sleeve.

"At first I put all my confidence in her prayers, I guess. But as I grew older, I knew I could talk to God myself. And I have. I suppose that's part of what eventually led me in the direction of the ministry. I wanted to be like Mrs. Bennett—always helping people, especially the kind of people no one else cared about."

"I think many of us understand," Michael replied. "I'm not a preacher, I'm a school counselor, and largely through Ophelia Bennett's influence, God has become the center of my life."

As others nodded or spoke up about Mrs. Bennett's influence, Boy waited. Then he said, "About two months ago, Mrs. Bennett called me long distance. My church is only about fifteen miles from where she lived. Since her retirement, she's been living in Benton Harbor. Do you know why there's a retirement center there? Just like the person she was back at North Prairie, she helped organize one."

"I'll bet it was well organized," Max Waxman said. "That's the way she was."

Boy nodded. "Yep, that's the way she was." He took out his handkerchief and wiped his tear-stained face. "She called me and asked me to come and see her. She knew then she was dying."

Then Boy Masters told the story.

*

Ophelia, fully dressed, lay on her bed. Slowly she pulled herself to a sitting position. She motioned for Boy to help her and he placed two large pillows behind her head and shoulders. "It is an extreme effort for me to talk loudly, so please sit close."

Boy pulled up a chair and sat as close to her bed as possible. "I love you, Mrs. Bennett." He took her hand and held it gently.

"I have loved you all these years, too. Oh, I have been proud of you—proud of all my students in all the schools where I have taught." Sadness filled her eyes. "Perhaps not all. Except for—for those who hurt my late husband—and even some of them, most of them, were fine students." She closed her eyes. "But especially I have been proud of the North Prairie students. I knew—I absolutely knew—that each of you would turn out well."

For several minutes she reminisced about that school year of 1940–41. She also mentioned various bits of information from those who had written regularly through the years. Every Christmas most of them sent a card or a letter; some mailed her an occasional note during the year. "A few of them phoned from time to time, and oh, how much I have cherished—" She stopped midsentence. "I do not expect to attend the reunion."

"Of course you'll make it. Who could stop you?"

"God."

He laughed. "But that's also the same source who will help you make it."

"I would like very much, yes, very much indeed, to attend the reunion, but I do not expect to be alive then. My heart condition has worsened. I had another bad attack three days ago. The doctor says I have been living by an extension of God's grace for the past year."

"I—I don't know what to say."

"Do not say anything. I have written a letter for the students." Breathing heavily, she reached over to the nightstand, opened a drawer, pulled out a sheaf of pages, and handed them to him. "As part of the letter, I have also included a brief message—a paragraph or two—for each of my former students. That is, I did for those who are still alive. Marvin Bagnull died last year. You knew that, didn't you?"

"Yes, and I knew about Ginger Garrett's death—what? five years ago?"

"Yes, something like that. Her car was hit by a drunk driver." She sighed. "I felt such a loss. She turned out to be a fine woman. Did you know she taught drama at Iowa State University? I miss her—even yet."

At a loss for words, he nodded.

"So I have written a letter—not a lot of words, but it begins with a short message to say to all of you how proud I have been of you through the years. You see, no matter how difficult my situation became—and especially after Richard died—I could always lean on the promise that God gave me back in 1940."

"What promise?"

"It is in the letter."

Boy turned the fifteen sheets of paper over and over in his hands. "What if you are able to come?"

"I will not be able to."

"But please, if you are able—"

"Then return the letter to me at the reunion." She laughed softly. "But I suggest you plan to read it to them."

"Okay—I guess so."

"And one more thing. When I die, I want you to conduct my funeral."

He exhaled. "I don't know if I could do that. I don't think I could hold up. You've been such a special person, I—"

"You can do it. In the office here at the retirement home they have my written instructions for everything. I should like to leave this world knowing that one of my students stood at the grave site." She pressed his hand. The strength of her grip amazed him. "I have always loved you, Boy, but through each of these years that love and admiration has grown as I have watched you mature. I would not want anyone else to do the funeral."

Boy stared at his feet, not wanting Ophelia Bennett to see the tears that demanded release. He knew his voice would crack if he tried to speak. He nodded and returned the pressure on her hand.

The two sat in silence and she relaxed in her bed. He held her hand until she drifted into sleep. Then he quietly left the room.

*

"I want to read the letter now," Boy said to his former classmates.

Yvonne still held Michael's hand. Her grip had tightened as if she feared what she might hear. A piped-in operatic aria by Maria Callas wafted into the room.

After a warm greeting to them all, Boy read a lengthy paragraph about every student. Ophelia Bennett reminded each one how he or she had behaved that first day of school and the changes that had come about before the year ended. Then she referred to the career paths they had taken—all of them in what she referred to as the helping professions.

The fifteen, hand-written pages concluded with these words:

> "In the fall of 1940, I did not want to teach at North Prairie School. It was not the discipline problem that deterred me, because I had enough confidence that I could handle that. I prayed for a long time and begged God to give me a different path to follow. In the end, I knew—in a way that one can only know by hearing the quiet, inner voice of God—that I would be your teacher and that we would form a special relationship, a relationship that would last a lifetime.
>
> "God promised me that I would be His voice to you. I am sure you remember my explaining that—or attempting to. God also gave me one other promise. I began to teach at North Prairie School with the divine assurance that each of you, in your own way and at the proper time, would follow God's path for your life. Not only that you would become staunch and faithful followers, but I had the assurance that God would

use your lives to change other lives.

"Is it not wonderful for you to know that God planned your future before we ever met? I was merely a divine instrument and I consider myself blessed to have been that instrument. Today you are teachers, therapists, coaches, doctors, and even one ordained minister.

"You make me proud to have been your teacher, to have served as part of the conduit to bring you to God. That promise is what kept my spirits up during those last weeks at North Prairie."

Boy's voice broke and he couldn't finish reading. Yvonne took the letter out of his hand and continued to read: "I have loved you very much, but God has always loved you more and bound us together."

For several minutes no one spoke. Each seemed lost in a personal recollection of Ophelia Bennett. Several cried quietly. Max doubled a fist as if he sought for something to strike. Then he dropped his hand and cried openly and without shame.

Finally Nickolas stood. "It's hard for me to believe Ophelia Bennett is dead. Somehow I think a person like her would live forever."

Edwina Forder stood. "She was the best—best friend—" Choked by her tears, she sat down.

Max stared straight ahead, his face glistening.

Karen took the hand of her husband, Nickolas, and when their eyes met, they embraced as tears flowed from both of them.

"We owe a lot to her," Larry said. "Her influence has helped make us what we are today. Certainly in my life that's true!"

Yvonne had been leaning forward, head in her hands. She slowly stood and looked at those sitting near her. "I ought to hate all of you. I would have if it hadn't been for Mrs. Bennett. Tonight I can honestly say that I love each of you. She was the person who taught me how to love. I was the poor girl, the outsider. You looked down on me—you never pretended not to—because I was Mexican and spoke poor English. Then she helped you to love me as well."

"We learned a lot from you," Michael said quietly.

"Then the thanks again goes to Mrs. Bennett. You know what I do for a living? I teach three languages besides English. But more than my proficiency, I'm a worthwhile person. I may not be the best I can be. I've failed so much. But I know that the promise came true, and I know that God is my friend."

"Mine, too," Max said almost inaudibly.

"I feel the same way," Larry said.

"So do I," added another voice.

"Because of Ophelia Bennett I'm able to say the same thing," Edwina said, although her voice was still shaky. "She not only influenced me through her prayers, but she taught me so much. For at least the next ten years after she left North Prairie, she constantly wrote to me. She shared new ideas and encouraged me to develop my own. I also know God as my friend."

"I—I need to say something," Michael said and stood. "I was a drunk for twelve years. I had thrown away my life and didn't care if I lived or died. Then one evening—the last night I had planned to stay on earth before taking my own life—she called me. Somehow she knew. 'Don't do it,' she said. 'I believe in you.' That's all she said before she hung up, but it was enough. I have never touched another drop of alcohol since then." He dropped his head, turned, and walked away as if he felt he didn't belong in the group.

"Don't!" Yvonne grabbed his hand and pulled him back. "All of us have stories of failures. But we also have tales of success—just like you."

Michael stared into the eyes of a woman that he had once disliked. Then he embraced her and held her tightly for several seconds. "I guess this is an example of what grace really is," he murmured.

Several others hugged Michael and spoke encouragingly to him.

"One more thing," Boy said. "At our church whenever anyone moves away, we have a special ceremony at the end of the worship hour. The last thing we do is sing 'Blest Be the Tie That Binds.' "

"Why, that's the same one we sang when Mrs. Bennett left," Carol said.

"That's why I made it a special part of the good-bye service at our church," Boy said. "For those of you who don't remember it, the first stanza goes like this," and he sang:

Blest be the tie that binds
Our hearts in Christian love;
The fellowship of kindred minds
Is like to that above.

"Let's join hands and all sing that together," he said.

The former students, along with Edwina and Reginald, stood and formed a circle. They sang the song through. Boy called out the words to another stanza and they sang that also.

We share each other's woes
Each other's burdens bear,

And often for each other flows
The sympathizing tear.

"I was just thinking about two things," Max said. "First, Mrs. Bennett gave me a verse from the Bible to memorize: 'I can do all things through Christ which strengtheneth me.' Because of her I have repeated that verse almost every day of my life since she gave it to me. Even more important, I believe it. For the first time, I think I understood what the words of that hymn mean." Max laughed. "I'm the organist at our church and I must have played that song hundreds of times. But just now, as we sang them, I thought about what they mean."

"I feel the same way," Karen said. "I think I finally understood what Mrs. Bennett wanted to teach us."

"The song is about our being together, about unifying us, making us know the commonality we share," Max said. "But it's more, isn't it? For forty years we were really lucky people. Maybe I should say blessed. We had two ties. First, we all had the prayers of Ophelia Bennett behind every one of us. Those prayers turned us to God. Now we all we have that divine love binding us together."

"Oh, yes, that's right," Karen said. "I'm going to miss that wonderful woman. Sometimes Nickolas and I had problems and we'd get discouraged. One thing that always kept me going was knowing that Mrs. Bennett prayed for me—for us—every day."

"Karen would call her," Nickolas said. "We didn't even have to tell her our problems. It was if she—well, she just knew. She wouldn't say a lot but without fail—"

"That's right!" Karen said. "Mrs. Bennett always knew exactly what to say and—"

"And she saved our marriage," Nickolas said.

"I felt the same way about her guidance," Carol said. "She knew—she always knew—as if she had some direct line to heaven that I didn't understand."

"Yes, me, too, and that wasn't only when I was a drunk," Michael said. "During these last three years, I don't think I would have held on to my faith if it hadn't been for her." He took a deep breath and said in a low voice, "My wife died of breast cancer and a week later my oldest son was killed in a traffic accident. Mrs. Bennett wrote me a letter every week. She never missed once. That went on for more than a year. I'd feel as if I couldn't make it another day. Then she'd call or I'd have a letter in the mail. How would I have made it without her letters and her prayers? That's what pulled me through. She represented God to me in a way that no other human being had before."

"Yes, yes, that's how I feel also," Yvonne said. "She did represent God to us. Oh, she wasn't perfect or anything like that, but I used to think of her as a special angel that heaven sent just for me. When I went through a very difficult time in my life—something only God and Mrs. Bennett knew about—I felt as if the Holy Spirit touched me and guided me back on the right path again. Through her I received so many words of comfort, of encouragement—"

"Now she's gone," Karen said.

"But we're not," Boy answered. "We're here. And we're all living the promise given by Ophelia Bennett."

"Hey, that's right," Nickolas said. "Because of her, we're all on the right path, aren't we?"

"What do we do now?" Max asked. "Our lives haven't stopped, but...well, I feel it's as if—"

"As if we can't let this stop with us? That we have to go on?" Karen asked.

"Something like that," he said. "Why did she do this? Why us? What are we supposed to do now?"

"Why don't we promise to pray for each other every day?" Yvonne said. "The way Ophelia Bennett did for us?"

"I think it would be what she'd like," Boy said.

"Yes, I think it would," Yvonne agreed.

"I'm all for it," Michael said.

"I'm all for it, but, I'm not sure I would be faithful," Yvonne said. "At least not like Mrs. Bennett."

"I have an idea," Michael said. "What would it be like if each of us chose one or two people, someone we see regularly—a child, an older person or—"

"You mean someone who needs love the way we did?" Yvonne asked. "Someone like that girl with the patched dress who walked into the classroom, feeling ugly and unloved?"

"Yes! That's exactly what I mean." Michael stared into Yvonne's eyes. "Is it too late to apologize for the way we treated you? For the way I personally treated you?"

"I forgave all of you a long, long time ago," she said.

Michael took her hand and this time he didn't release it.

"If we did something like that," Karen said, "you know, looking for those people who are hurting, who are as bad off as we were—why, I think Mrs. Bennett would smile down from heaven."

"Then the promise of Ophelia Bennett wouldn't really end, would it?" Max asked. "It would be our way to carry it on—to love, to help, to—"

"To serve God, but also to enrich our lives," Boy said. "We can't forget that. We gained so much from her prayers. Our prayers can enrich others. We might even be used to change lives."

"We depended on her for so many years," Nickolas said. "Maybe it is time for us to continue the spirit of Ophelia Bennett in the world. Maybe it's time for us to become instruments of divine love."

"Especially to those who need love the most," Yvonne added.

"And those who deserve it the least," Michael added. "Like the rotten bunch of kids at North Prairie."

"How many of you want to do it?" Max asked.

Every hand shot up.

"I want in on this," Reginald said. "And so does Edwina. You know, Mrs. Bennett included me in her prayers. We corresponded regularly, and we named our oldest daughter Ophelia. Mrs. Bennett wasn't my teacher, but she was my friend."

"We all agree then? Every one of us?" Nickolas asked as they all nodded or replied affirmatively.

"That way the promise of Ophelia Bennett lives on, doesn't it?" Karen said.

"When we asunder part," Max began singing, his baritone voice rising in volume as the others joined him, "it gives us inward pain; but we shall all be joined in heart and hope to meet again."

The surviving thirty-one former students joined hands and included Reginald and Edwina Forder. They sang the stanza through a second time. When they finished, no one moved, as though reluctant to break the unity of the moment.

"Please, may we sing it one more time?" Yvonne asked. "Let's sing it this time for Mrs. Bennett as praise to God for her life."

Max began once again and their voices rose to a crescendo.

Acknowledgments

Special thanks for my family, beginning with the late Cornelia Brackett, my wife's mother, my good friend, and a wonderful teaching mentor to me.

Wanda Rosenberry (our daughter) and my wife, Shirley, believed in this book and encouraged me to write it. Thank you both.

And special thanks to Ramona Tucker. I was ready to send the manuscript into oblivion. She asked to read it, liked it, and offered me a contract.

Real. Transparent. Honest. Gutsy. Straightforward.

UNLEASH
THE WRITER WITHIN

THE ESSENTIAL WRITERS' COMPANION

CECIL MURPHEY

Who You Are Determines What You Write.

You have unique stories to tell the world, teachings and words that will inspire and encourage others. So what are you waiting for? It's time to unleash that writer within.

This isn't your average writing book, with guilt-inducing lists of "how-tos" in your search to become a writer…or a better writer. Instead, internationally renowned and beloved writer Cecil Murphey walks as a companion alongside as you:

- Discover who you are.
- Develop your voice and writing style.
- Learn to write with heart.
- Become authentic to your readers.
- Grapple with the dreaded "Writer's Block" (it's not the deadly monster it seems).
- Harness the inner critic (and a few outer ones too).
- Expand your comfort zone.

The "must-have" resource for every writer.
The perfect "retreat in a book" for writers events, discussions, and conferences.

Lessons from a Lifetime of Writing

CECIL MURPHEY

If you want to become the best writer you can be,
Writer to Writer is for you.

This isn't a grammar book. It isn't a rulebook for writers. It's the "in the trenches" companion for you along your writing journey, whether you're just starting out or have been writing for years. In *Writer to Writer,* award-winning author and beloved mentor Cecil Murphey shares the lessons he's learned from a lifetime of writing. Read one of the bite-sized entries a day, a chapter a week, or the entire book at once. Jump into the book any place you like. It's also a handy discussion tool for writing groups.

Topics include:
*how to look like a professional (even if you're an amateur)
*writing basics you need to know
*fine-tuning your fiction
*how to keep your reader intrigued
*what annoys and pleases publishers
*dealing with writers' block and rejections
*tips for writers groups
*literary agents and contracts
*making a living as a writer

and much more.

Writer to Writer is...

The Must-Have Resource for Every Writer.

"Good writing demands self-discipline and constant learning. I'm still learning. In the meanwhile, *Writer to Writer* is my legacy gift to you. I want to help you become a better writer."

—CECIL MURPHEY

www.cecwritertowriter.com
www.cecilmurphey.com
www.oaktara.com

*

New York Times' bestselling author and international speaker **Cecil (Cec) Murphey** has written or co-written more than 130 books, including the runaway bestseller *90 Minutes in Heaven* (with Don Piper) and *Gifted Hands: The Ben Carson Story* (with Dr. Ben Carson). His books have sold millions of copies, been translated into more than 40 languages, and brought hope and encouragement to countless people around the world. See **www.cecilmurphey.com** for more information. For writing tips and advice, visit **www.cecwritertowriter.com.**

About the Author

CECIL ("CEC") MURPHEY can't recall when he didn't want to write. Although he tried to get published first at age 16, he had nothing accepted until he was 38—"only after I'd learned a few things about the publishing industry," he says.

After Cec sold at least 20 articles, he made a double commitment to God and to himself: never to stop learning and improving as a writer, and to do whatever he could to help other writers. Thus began a lifetime commitment and passion to share with other writers what he's learned along the way. *Unleash the Writer Within* and *Writer to Writer* are his passions and legacies to all writers in the trenches.

"I wrote *The Promises of Ophelia Bennett* because I taught in a two-room private school for a year with my wife's mother, Cornelia Brackett," Cec says. "I learned so much about teaching from her, and some of those lessons appear in this novel."

Since his writing career launched, Cec has written or co-written more than 130 books, including the *New York Times'* bestseller *90 Minutes in Heaven* (with Don Piper) and *Gifted Hands: The Ben Carson Story* (with Dr. Ben Carson). His books have sold millions of copies, been translated into more than 40 languages, and brought hope and encouragement to countless people around the world. Cecil Murphey enjoys speaking for churches and for events nationwide. For more information, or to contact him, visit his website at **www.cecilmurphey.com.**

Cecil's blog for male survivors of sexual abuse:
www.menshatteringthesilence.blogspot.com.

Cecil's blog for writers: **www.cecwritertowriter.com.**

www.oaktara.com